Myster

To Abby
Sleep Well
Mary M. Cushnie-Mansour

A Collection of Short Stories

to keep you up at night--

Reading!

Other Works by Mary M. Cushnie-Mansour

Night's Vampire Series

Night's Gift
Night's Children
Night's Return
Night's Temptress
Night's Betrayals (Coming in 2017)

Children's Novels

A Story of Day & Night

Children's English/French Story Books
The *Just Imagine Children's Series*

The Day Bo Found His Bark
Jesse's Secret
Freddy Frog's Frolic (Coming in Summer 2016)
The Tempter Tantrum (Coming in Summer 2016)

Short Stories

From the Heart

Biographies

A 20th Century Portia

Poetry

Life's Roller Coaster
Devastations of Mankind
Shattered
Memories

Mysteries from the Keys

A Collection of Short Stories

By

Mary M. Cushnie-Mansour

CAVERN
OF DREAMS
PUBLISHING

Mysteries From the Keys

Ordering Information:
Books may be ordered directly through the Publisher's website: www.cavernofdreams.com

Cavern of Dreams Publishing
43 Kerr-Shaver Terrace
Brantford, ON N3T 6H8
1-519-770-7515

Library and Archives Canada Cataloguing in Publication

Cushnie-Mansour, Mary M., 1953-, author
Mysteries from the keys : a collection of short stories / Mary M. Cushnie Mansour.

Short stories.
Issued in print and electronic formats.
ISBN 978-1-927899-39-7 (paperback).--ISBN 978-1-927899-41-0 (html)

I. Title.

PS8605.U83M97 2016 C813'.6 C2016-901351-0
C2016-901352-9

It is only through mystery and madness that the soul is revealed--Thomas Moore

The true mystery of the world is the visible, not the invisible--Oscar Wilde

Acknowledgements

When a writer writes, there are so many people they are obliged to. First, are the individuals who listen to the various drafts of genius scribbled upon the pages, and who offer honest critiques despite the author's pout and stamping of feet. Secondly, and some of these individuals overlap with the first group, are family members who have tolerated lapses in domestic duties while the writer created their masterpieces. I know, my husband has suffered the lack of proper meals at times, and periodically, the absence of clean laundry—yet he still supports my dreams.

To speak to those individually, though, to this particular book, I would like to thank the readers of my short story column that I used to write for the Brantford Expositor. Most of the mystery stories in this book appeared in my column, and the feedback from my fans was heart-warming and most encouraging.

A special thank you goes out to Heather and Angie of Lock & Key Treasures in Brantford for allowing me to come into their store to do a photo shoot for my cover art.

And, not to be forgotten, where would I be if I did not have Terry Davis from Ball Media in Brantford to put the finishing touches on my cover. Once again, another job well done!

A writer must never forget to thank their editors: Danielle Tanguay and Bethany Jamieson of Cavern of Dreams Publishing, who did an excellent job of pointing out some issues in the stories that needed fine-tuning.

There are a number more people I could personally thank here, but I will finish up with Randy Nickmann of Brant Service Press for his support and printing of my books.

To anyone I have not thanked by name—friends and fans of my work—you know who you are, and I want you to know your support is appreciated from the bottom of my heart.

Table of Contents

frétille un printemps encore ! gaiment
elles sont blanches, il neige des fleurs. Regardez les

Minnie's Way

Minnie still lived in the house where she was born, and it was showing its age the same as she—especially in the frosty winter months. Skeletal trees tapped nervously on the wooden shingles. Flecks of paint would occasionally dance with the snowflakes when the wind pressured the timber walls. The lofty, wooden pillars, placed to support an overhang that covered a wrap-around veranda, were faltering. The front door was encircled by six diamond eyes that pierced the perimeters of their view. Satin curtains clouded the picture of what might be beyond the glass.

Inside, Minnie sat in her oak rocker, rocking and humming long-ago tunes. Her eyes were closed; however, it would not matter if she opened them for they had not seen the light for many years.

Dover, an old yellow lab, lay at her feet. A black cat, a stray Minnie had never called anything other than "Cat," lounged on the grubby couch. Walking paths, resembling a fox-and-rabbit game in the snow, meandered through the thick dust on the sitting room floor. Candle wax created various figurines on the end tables, coffee table, and dining table. A phonograph sat silently in the far corner, an old 45 on the turntable—void of dust.

Footsteps approached the door. Dover wagged his tail, a sign he sensed a friend. Minnie heard the tail thump on the floor and smelled the particles of dust as they were disturbed. A familiar voice called out: "Minnie, I'm coming in now."

Dover's tail beat harder. Cat opened her eyes halfway. Minnie kept rocking. The door creaked open. "I must remember to bring some oil with me tomorrow," the voice mentioned as its owner entered the room. "Are you hungry, Minnie? What a silly question. Of course, you must be; probably haven't eaten yet, eh?" The voice disappeared in the direction of the kitchen.

Minnie smiled. It had been a good breakfast, but she wouldn't tell—some things were best left unsaid.

"How about a nice poached egg?" The sound of the fridge door opening reached Minnie's ears. "Hmmmmm—guess I should have stopped for groceries—I thought there were plenty of eggs here yesterday. Are you holding out on me, Minnie? Have you been entertaining? No, of course not; how silly of me." The fridge door closed.

Minnie smiled.

The voice entered the parlour. "I need to run to the grocer; I'll be right back…you want anything special…of course not…you never do…"

Minnie smiled.

The front door opened and closed.

Minnie stood, retrieved her cane, and tapped her way along the trail to peek through the diamond eyes—an old habit. She was comforted by the sound of her old friends tapping on the roof. Dover walked close to her. Cat didn't move from the couch.

Minnie smiled and secured the lock in place. Ginny never asked how the door was locked and unlocked between errands, showing how much she paid attention to little details. It was just a job for her—she wasn't like Nigel. Nigel had been Minnie's butler for years, taking good care of her after her mother and father were killed in a horrible automobile accident. But he had passed away a couple of years ago, leaving her at the mercy of the system.

Minnie turned and took the path over to the phonograph. Dover followed. She reached for the needle, placed it on the record, and then turned the handle. Music filtered up and out of the horn, and Minnie began to sway to the old jazz tune. Cat decided to join them. She meandered over and jumped up on the yellow keys of the upright piano that sat beside the phonograph. A medley of off notes soured the song that was playing. Minnie's brow furrowed.

"Scat, Cat," she ordered.

Cat ignored her. As the echo died away, Minnie forgot about Cat and continued with her dance, taking tiny steps, with her arms in waltz position, and her head turned up and to the side. Dover moved out of the way and sat beside the piano bench. He and Cat had spent many hours watching this ritual.

Time was forgotten. "Yes, Nigel…not so tight, Nigel…what would Father say…he would not be pleased with your intimacy with me…oh, yes, you are right, Mother always loved you…" Minnie laughed. "Oh, how I love it when you twirl me so…your arms are so strong…no, I cannot marry you; Father wouldn't approve…we shall just have to continue like this…promise you'll never leave me…promise me, Nigel…"

The music stopped.

Cat jumped down and returned to the couch; Dover led the way back to the rocking chair. The key turned in the door, and Ginny entered with a bag of groceries. She looked around the room; all was as it should be.

Minnie smiled. Dover thumped his tail. Cat closed her eyes.

The Storm

What a miserable day. The rain hasn't stopped, and the temperature is dropping rapidly. This means everything will freeze and the roads will be exceptionally hazardous.

My cat is acting downright weird today, too. Not that she isn't naturally weird, but today, she just keeps running from one window to the next. She even knocked over the one houseplant I have managed to keep alive. Oh well, the poor plant was on its way out anyway.

Lightning flashed across the sky, and thunder boomed on its heel. The phone rang. Who the heck would be calling at this ungodly hour of ten o'clock at night, I wondered as I checked my watch. All my friends know better than to call my house past nine fifty-nine.

"Hello," I said, picking up the receiver.

A raspy voice was on the other end of the line. "Have you checked your barn in the last couple of hours?"

"Who is this?" I demanded to know.

"Just answer the question, lady."

"Not until you answer mine," I insisted.

"What a pretty horse you have, lady," the voice rasped on. "Is he still in the barn?"

I plopped down in the chair beside the phone. I started to shake. "What do you mean…is my horse still in the barn?" I shouted, fear welling up in my chest.

"Look, lady, get the picture: I have your horse, and I want you to put one hundred thousand dollars in a sealed envelope and drop it off by the old mission cross out on West 99th Street. Do you know the place I'm talking about?"

"Yes." I was too dumbstruck to say anything further.

"Good, have the money there by six p.m. tomorrow, or you will never see your horse again!" The receiver clicked shut before I could declare poverty.

I stood and began to pace. Where the hell am I going to get one hundred thousand dollars by tomorrow? Who's playing this sick joke on me? I'd sunk every penny I had into buying the beautiful Arab stallion, Alejandro, and I was hoping to earn back some of my investment by studding him out. He had a pedigree longer than my arm.

I wondered if it was Mr. Gunner. He had wanted Alejandro for himself, but I had outbid him at the auction. I remembered the ugly look on his face as I led Alejandro up to my trailer.

"Too much horse for you, missy," he'd shouted at me.

"We'll see," I'd retorted back. I had never liked Mr. Gunner. Actually, no one liked him. He had a bad reputation in the horse world. He was mean to his horses, so the stories told.

I picked up the phone to call the police, but I hung up before dialling. I needed to check the barn first. I grabbed my coat and headed out the door.

The wind hit me hard. The rain, which had turned to sleet, burned my exposed skin. I was running in the direction of the barn, but it wasn't there. I became hysterical, running in circles. It started to snow. Drifts were appearing everywhere, encircling me. I tried to make my way back to the house. I couldn't find it.

Then, I heard a loud crash. I slid on some ice, and I was falling…falling…bang…bump… Meeeeoooww!

My eyes opened. I was on the floor beside my bed. The cat was charging out of the room. I picked myself up off the floor and headed to the bathroom. I was sopping wet. I took a towel and wiped the sweat from my face.

"Thank God, it was just a dream," I mumbled to the empty room.

I went to the window and gazed out at the weather. Looked like the rain was turning into sleet—we were most likely in for an ice storm. I turned to go back to bed.

The phone rang. I let it ring seven or eight times before picking up the receiver. After all, it was after ten o'clock.

"Hello," I said, slowly.

A raspy voice was on the other end of the line. "Have you checked your barn in the last couple of hours?"

The receiver crashed to the floor.

We Can Smile Again

There is a part of me that wishes it never happened; yet, the satisfied part of me cannot help but to smile. Sylvia smiles, as well. And she dances, too—like a mad fairy.

I grew up in the small town of Waterford. Sylvia moved next door when we were the tender age of thirteen. She was from Hamilton, and I was enthralled the "big city girl" paid attention to me. We became best friends, and our friendship has survived for we share secrets that are buried in our hearts' darkest corners.

There was madness in Sylvia's eyes—her mother's, too. In fact, when Sylvia had shown me some old family pictures, everyone had the same look. One thing I had noticed was there were no males in the photos. I never thought to ask Sylvia about that, though.

Sylvia and I did not play the silly games girls of thirteen participated in. We had a secret place. It was secluded in a grove of trees on top of a hill. It had been the servants' quarters of the old Cooper house Sylvia and her mother now lived in. I spent hours, with pen and paper, creating imaginary worlds. Sylvia shaped her clay and danced. We were content. Life was good.

Sometimes, we would sit by one of the windows and peek at the outside world. We'd smile at each other as we observed the other teens playing at being adults, and then we'd return to our work—I, to my pages; Sylvia, to her clay.

Then came the summer of Samwell. He arrived from Mexico to work in the tobacco fields, and we were caught unprepared for his devastating charms—especially did he catch

Sylvia. I would go to our secret place and find the door bolted. I would knock, but there was never an answer. Baffled, I'd walk back down the path, sit by the oak tree, and wait. She would tire of him soon—she'd never favour him above our friendship—I was sure of that.

When we did have time together, I noticed Sylvia seemed absorbed with other things, none of which she confided in me. She'd just walk dazedly around the room, trailing her fingers over the dusty pottery.

Samwell always seemed to lurk nearby whenever I was with Sylvia, which irked me. I would observe him leaning against the old oak tree, a cigarette dangling from his mouth and a smirk on his face as he stared up at the shack. It was as though he was just waiting for me to leave so he could move in.

When we came down the hill, Sylvia would walk past him, but I observed the obscene body language between them. Once in my house, I took to going directly to my bedroom, where I would watch from my window. Sylvia always raced back to the oak tree—to *him.*

I cried a lot that summer, waiting for the tobacco harvest to be over. Samwell would go home then and my friend would return to me. I would exonerate her of the transgression against our friendship, just as I was sure Sylvia would have exonerated me had I made a mistake.

Summer took her leave; fall strutted in with glorious, rustic colours. The tobacco workers began to disappear from our streets. But, Samwell did not leave. Then, one day, Sylvia brought me the boxes that contained my writings. Her eyes were crazy as she handed them to me.

"Samwell missed his plane home and won't be able to get another flight for a month or two. The airline won't refund his money, so he has to get a job to buy another ticket. He will be able to save quicker if he doesn't have to pay rent, so I said he could stay up on the hill. I don't want him to poke through your stories. You can return when he's gone."

That was it. Sylvia just left and headed back up the hill to "our secret place." I carried the boxes to my room, walked to my window, watched my friend disappear up the hill, and cried—again.

Sylvia began missing school. When she did show up, there was an awkward silence between us. The magic of the past three years was gone.

"When is he leaving?" I asked on one of those days.

"Why?"

"Well, it has been a month; November is almost here and the weather is going to get worse. Not paying rent, I just thought he might have saved enough for his plane ticket by now."

"He did, but he sent his mother the money to buy medicine for his little brother."

"Doesn't she want him to come home?"

"Not really. Besides, there is nothing there for him. He might stay here…what are you looking so glum about…at least, he has a job."

"But he can't stay up there!" I spoke sharply.

She grabbed my arm and swung me around to face her. "Give me one good reason why not!" Her eyes were gleaming madly.

"Ouch!" I pulled away. "What's going on, Sylvia? I thought we were friends—that is supposed to be our place. I thought Samwell was temporary! What is happening to you?" I burst into tears.

"Sorry if I've hurt you, Carey, but as great grandmama used to say, life moves on, and so do people."

Her answer cut my heart. "So…this means you are moving on?"

"Yes." She got up and left the school. I knew where she was headed—without me. As I watched her leave, I noticed the change in her movement—her feet did not dance as they had a few short months ago. It was at that point I knew something was drastically wrong!

Eventually, Sylvia was kicked out of school. She gathered together her few possessions and then dropped her pens on my desk. "Here," she murmured, "you have more use for these than I." She shuffled slowly from the room, her shoulders slumped, her steps heavy.

I wanted to confront Samwell and demand to know what he was doing to her. To ask why there were black circles around her eyes…why her back was hunched so…why her feet did not dance anymore? I needed to save my friend.

I watched their comings and goings. I saw a difference in his walk, too. He would stagger up the hill, bumping from tree to tree, falling on the path—probably from drinking too much. I feared, more than ever, for Sylvia's safety. I prayed for a night when my parents would go out so I could go up to the shack and find out what was happening.

Finally, the perfect night unfolded. My parents were invited to a 25th wedding anniversary house party for some old friends, and an October pea soup fog had rolled in. The Marshalls lived in the country and had insisted their guests stay over. Mom called, instructed me to lock everything up and go to bed. I had Mrs. Winter's phone number in case of an emergency.

I smiled, headed to my room, dragged my rocker over to the window, and sat down. Samwell would be along soon and my eyes would have to be sharp to see through the blasted fog.

My alarm clock ticked softly. I kept shaking off sleep. I needed some music…the deep notes beat in my veins.

Time passed.

The music stopped.

Silence, but for the ticking clock.

Sleep…

"Damn!" I jumped up; it was one-thirty.

I had probably missed Samwell's return, but I needed to go up there anyway and put an end to whatever was going on.

I shoved my feet into my runners, grabbed my jacket and house key, and ran downstairs. I almost tripped over the Halloween pumpkin by the back door. Outside, the fog closed in around me, penetrating the fabric, dampening my skin—or was that nervous sweat?

I could have gone up that pathway blindfolded, I had travelled it so many times. As I drew closer to the shack, I noticed a candle trembling in the window. I heard loud noises from the inside, and then, I heard the ugliest voice.

"You witch! Where's the money?" There was a loud slapping sound, but no whimper followed.

"Tell me!" the voice roared.

"Go to hell and fry!" a female voice screamed. Then, there was another slapping sound, followed by a crash.

I moved quickly to the door and with all my valour, I burst into the room. Sylvia was cowered beneath a table. She was half naked, her clothing tattered and torn. Bruises and bloody scratches played snakes and ladders on the exposed skin. But her eyes held a fiery madness like I had never seen before! She was glaring at Samwell with such hatred that even he momentarily stopped his assault.

I seized the moment and grabbed the fire poker by the door—the one Sylvia and I kept there in case any unwanted strangers tried to invade our world.

This was our secret place—Sylvia's and mine.

Samwell was unwanted.

I swung with all my might.

The clay felt pleasant to my trembling fingers. Sylvia showed me how to smooth and shape it. "You can create anything you want with clay," she smiled.

We worked all night on the new piece. In the morning, I ran down to my house and left a note for my parents, informing them that Sylvia and I were sleeping in the shack and I would see them tomorrow. We slept for a few hours and then continued our work. Finally, we sat back and observed our creation. He was magnificent, just like when we had first seen him.

"Not bad, for a beginner," Sylvia smiled. She began to dance around the sculpture. "You know what…I think we will enter this in the Pumpkin Fest pottery show. There is a new category this year: 'Real Life Creations.'"

"I could write a story to go with it, an amalgamation of two arts," I added with a smile.

"Good idea." And Sylvia smiled again.

The town of Waterford is proud of their world renowned artist and writer. Sylvia inherited her mother's property when her mother passed away. We live in the main house, however, we still spend a lot of time in our secret place. We fixed the walls and broken windows. We also expanded the shack by adding two rooms—one where I write my manuscripts, one where Sylvia works her magic with clay.

However, it is our statues and the stories that go with them that have truly made us famous. Sylvia and I won the grand prize with our first entry ten years ago. We win first prize every year, and after each show, we add another statue to our iron-fenced garden on the hill. The stories are encased in a glass box beside their inspirations.

At the moment, we are working on another statue, one of the most exquisite we have ever executed. Unfortunately, it will not be ready for this year's show, for the clay is too fresh, and I have yet to write the story.

There is a part of me that wishes it had never happened, yet the satisfied part of me cannot help but to smile. Sylvia smiles, as well. And she dances, too—like a mad fairy—in the garden of statues.

Closing the Cottage

It had been a long summer. Mom and dad were heading back to the city and to their mundane jobs. She would be staying for another six weeks, being of an age now—nineteen—that her parents were not hesitant to leave her. She smiled; she'd been waiting a long time for this opportunity.

"Caroline, we're leaving now, love," her mom called up the stairs.

"Be down in a sec," Caroline shouted.

"Your father has the car running, dear; please don't dawdle."

"I won't, Mother." Caroline's eyes squinted—she hated to be pressured. She pushed her chair away from the computer; no need to turn it off today because she, and her cat, Princess, would be the only ones in the cottage after *they* left.

"Caro…"

"Here, Mother," Caroline shouted as she bounded down the stairs.

"Careful, dear, you'll fall."

"Where's Dad?" Caroline asked, ignoring her mother's concern.

"In the car."

"He couldn't wait in here to say goodbye to me?"

"He wants to leave before the traffic gets too heavy; you know how he hates driving bumper to bumper."

"He should have thought of that before he bought this place way up here in cottage heaven!" Caroline said with a sneer in her voice.

"He bought it for you, dear, to help you recover from your breakdown."

"He did?"

"Yes, and it did help you…the peace and quiet of the area…the lake. You love going out on the water in the boat, and swimming in the early morning and at sunset. I think it helped, keeping you away from the city's summer hustle. "

"Did it?" Caroline smirked, and then laughed. "Oh, Mother, give me a hug and a kiss; I won't be seeing you for a while."

Mother and daughter embraced. "Are you sure you'll be okay, dear?"

"I'll be fine," Caroline sighed, pulling out of the embrace.

"Don't forget, Mr. Malcolm is just across the lake. He can be here in a jiffy with that boat of his. Just call him on the CB."

"I'll be fine, Mother." Caroline didn't like Mr. Malcolm—he gave her the creeps.

"If you take our boat into town, make sure you leave early enough so you can return before nightfall. It gets dark early now and…"

"Mother, we've gone over all this. Stop worrying, I'll be OK. You better hurry or Dad will leave you behind, and then you'll get fired from your job for not showing up!" Caroline laughed as she headed out the door.

Her father was in the car, impatiently tapping the steering wheel. "Good-bye, Dad."

"Oh, finally…good-bye, Caroline; is your mother coming? We're going to miss the ferry to the mainland."

Caroline winced. "Of course…she was just giving me last minute instructions—again."

Caroline's mother scurried into the car. "Sorry, Gerry, I was just going over things with Caroline and…"

"Buckle up, Lucy." Gerry put the car into drive. "See you in a few weeks, kiddo; take care of yourself." The car sped off down the lane way.

Caroline waved to her mother, who would keep waving until the car disappeared around the bend. Mother was always pokey, something she couldn't help. Caroline had figured that out before she had turned ten years old.

Caroline headed back into the cottage. She plugged in the kettle to boil water for a pot of tea. Princess came out of hiding and began rubbing around her legs. Caroline checked the cat dish—it was empty. She filled it with kibble.

Princess pushed Caroline's hand away with her nose and began chomping on the kibble. Her tail puffed and she started purring.

Caroline poured a cup of tea and buried her nose in the fragrant steam. Peach was her favourite. She locked the front and back doors and then checked all the windows to ensure they were closed and locked, as well. There was a chill in the air this morning. With everything in good order, she headed up to her room.

The screensaver had settled in on the laptop computer. Mystical creatures: unicorns, dragons, fairies, and vampires travelled across the screen, camouflaging what was beneath them. Caroline set her tea cup down, moved the mouse and smiled as she read the words on the screen…

> *"Finally, they are gone," Ruth murmured under her breath…"*

Princess jumped on the desk, settling on a stack of papers. Caroline began to type…

> *…how she hated always playing 'the game'…now, they would all have to play hers—especially Mr. M., who lived across the lake.*

> *Ruth looked around. She had secured everything in place: the traps…the notes...the plan...the room. She slipped on her jacket and stepped into the crisp morning air. She wanted to check the traps. It would be weeks before anyone ventured up this way again.*
>
> *It was not a fruitful morning. The traps were empty. Ruth was sure Mr. M. didn't suspect anything—what was there to suspect? He figured he had everyone fooled—but not her—she read right through him—she knew what he was capable of...*

Caroline typed throughout the afternoon. The story was taking shape in her computer. Princess occasionally cracked open an eye, making sure her mistress hadn't deserted her. Finally, Caroline pushed away from the keyboard. "Time to get something to eat, kitty." She scratched Princess behind the ears.

The sun was beginning to disappear behind the pines.

Caroline opened the fridge, pulled out some leftover lasagne, popped it in the oven, and then headed down to the basement. Her father had purchased some steel traps a couple of summers ago because they'd had a raccoon infestation. Her mother had protested, so he'd gone out and bought some *humane cages* to appease her. Caroline knew her father had used the traps anyway; she'd followed him one day when he'd snuck out early in the morning. She followed him a lot—she'd seen a lot; learned a lot, too.

Her father was quite meticulous; one would never suspect the traps had ever been used. Caroline took them off their hooks, returned to the main floor, set the traps by the back door, and then pulled her supper from the oven. She glanced at the clock—only

4:30, but she needed to sleep early so she could wake early to accomplish what she had to do.

She took her supper out to the front veranda and sat in one of the Muskoka chairs. The sun had disappeared behind the tall fir trees that surrounded the lake. The water was tranquil. Caroline picked up her binoculars from the end table by the chair and focused on Mr. Malcolm's cottage. It was easy to see across the lake on a clear day, but if one wanted greater details, they had to use binoculars.

He was chopping and piling firewood. Apparently he lived there year round. There were stories about Mr. Malcolm, but Caroline's father thought that Mr. Malcolm was a good man. Caroline didn't get that feeling.

He paused in his work, turned, and stared over at her. Caroline shivered and headed back inside the cottage. She put the binoculars up to her eyes and watched Mr. Malcolm through the blinds until he resumed piling his wood. Then, she made sure the locks were fastened on the doors and windows and went upstairs to her room.

Princess was still sleeping on the desk. Caroline set her clothes out for the morning. She didn't want to have to turn on any lights—he might be watching. She flicked the television on just in time to catch the 6:00 news.

"A young woman has gone missing from the Lake District, the fourth one this summer. Cindy Logan was last seen, with her German Shepherd, Duke, heading off on some hiking trails. The dog returned to the campground around 5:00 this afternoon, without his mistress..."

Caroline flicked the television off. She reached under her bed, pulled out a scrapbook, and began flipping through the pages. Every summer since they'd owned this property, young women had been disappearing. She'd kept the newspaper articles and had made her own notes alongside each one. She also had some photos—ones she'd taken—photos that could be incriminating for a certain someone. She put the book back and lay down. The alarm clock was set for 4:00 a.m. She had no time to waste now that there was another victim!

The alarm buzzed loudly. Caroline bolted from bed, dressed, and headed downstairs. The moon cast a path of light through the kitchen window. She gathered up the traps and headed out the door.

The early morning whooping of the loons greeted her. Caroline clutched the traps close to her chest so they wouldn't rattle and then headed to where her canoe was tied to the dock. The motor boat was housed in the boathouse on the other side of the cottage. Caroline hated using it, so her dad had finally purchased a used canoe for her this past summer.

Caroline laid the traps in the canoe's belly and stepped in. She manoeuvred into a comfortable position and began to paddle. It took longer than she expected to cross the lake, despite its relative tranquillity. Finally, the canoe grated on the shore, just down from Mr. Malcolm's cottage. Caroline tied the canoe to a tree, gathered the traps, and headed for the woods that skirted his property. She had noticed him go there quite often. Sometimes her father went with him.

Just inside the trees, she saw a well-worn path that led to a marsh. A couple old camping chairs sat near the edge, a battered tin pail, filled with cigar butts, placed between them. Caroline surveyed her surroundings. She checked for footprints and then began setting the traps. Satisfied that at least one of them would do the job, she returned to her canoe.

Back in her cottage, Caroline made a pot of peppermint tea. Princess meandered around her legs, begging for breakfast.

Caroline filled her plate and then took her tea and headed up to her room. She turned the computer on and pulled up her story…

Ruth hadn't checked the traps for a couple of days—she'd come down with a terrible cold. She lay in bed wondering if she'd caught any prey. Her cat was curled at the foot of the bed, fast asleep. "I better check things out today," Ruth said to her cat. "I don't want anyone else to come upon any prey I may have caught…"

Caroline pushed her chair back as she noticed the time at the bottom of the computer screen—11:55. Her throat felt scratchy. Another pot of tea would be in order, she thought as she stood and headed downstairs. "Come on, Princess," she called to her sleeping cat. Princess flicked her ears and continued her nap on the foot of the bed.

Caroline decided on a cup of soup instead of tea. While her soup was heating in the microwave, she took the binoculars to the front window and looked over at Mr. Malcolm's cottage. All appeared quiet. Of course, he was most likely having his lunch, unless he had gotten caught up somewhere. The microwave timer beeped. Caroline smiled and set the binoculars down. It was probably safe to sit on the porch.

As Caroline sipped the soup, her mind wandered to the young woman, Cindy Logan, who had just gone missing. She also wondered about the other girls featured in her scrapbook. All of them had disappeared without a trace, as well.

She glanced across the lake. A thick fog was just beginning to roll in, but Caroline caught a glimpse of Mr. Malcolm on his front porch. He was staring over at *her*, and he waved. She just about spilled her soup in her haste to get inside the cottage. She clicked the lock into place. Caroline leaned back against the door and slid down to the floor. Princess came pattering down the stairs, headed for her dish, and began meowing.

"I just want this to be over," Caroline mumbled to her cat as she rubbed Princess behind the ears. "See you upstairs; I'm going to work on my story."

Caroline climbed the stairs to her room and sat down at the computer. She reached over and flicked on the desk light. The room was dark, the fog having closed a curtain on the afternoon sun. "Oh, Ruth, what shall you do now?" Caroline asked as she began to type…

Ruth prepared a TV dinner and took it down to the basement. She walked to the far end, stopped before a large steel door, took a key from her pocket and put it in the lock. The door swung open. Inside was dim; the only light filtering through was from a small, barred window. There was a stale human odour—male. A groan came from the far corner.

"Want your supper?" Ruth asked with a sneer in her voice.

Another groan.

"Speak up, I can't hear you!"

Another groan. Ruth leaned over the figure. "This ankle looks pretty bad; is it painful?" she asked, giving it a poke.

This time, the groan was filled with agony.

"Oh, forgive me—you can't talk with so much tape on your mouth. Here, let me help you with that!" Ruth reached over to the face and ripped the tape off.

The man screamed…

Princess jumped onto the desk and walked across the keyboard. “Silly cat,” Caroline said, scooping her off the desk and putting her on the floor.

Caroline’s throat was extremely sore now. Must have been the early morning dampness she had endured crossing the lake, and while setting the traps. She knew how susceptible she was to such weather, especially since her mental breakdown, which seems to have affected her immune system as well. She reached into her desk drawer, pulled out an Echinacea spray, and gave her throat a shot. She glanced at the computer time—5:00 already.

Caroline got up, turned her television on and lay down on the bed beside Princess. The early news was just beginning…

“No trace, whatsoever, of Cindy Logan,” the newscaster was saying. *“The search party has found no clues…”*

Caroline pulled her scrapbook out again and ran her fingers over the pictures of each of the girls—Traci Burns, Jordan Knowles, Karen Watson, Bernadette Holmes, Tammy Munst… She snapped the book shut, tears welling up in her eyes. She flicked the television off and headed downstairs. Princess followed.

Once in the kitchen, Caroline grabbed a set of keys from the drawer and headed down to the basement, walking past the humane animal traps, noticing the empty spot above them. At the end of the main room, she put a key into a large steel door and stepped inside another room. There was only one tiny window, with bars. Her father had fashioned this room so that it was fireproof in order to store important documents, but he never had. Why he’d made it so large, she could never figure out because she had actually never noticed that he had ever used the room. But for her purposes, it was just fine. Caroline flicked a light switch. All was in order—waiting…

As Caroline was walking back to the stairs, she heard a knock on the back door. It sounded desperate…

Princess was pacing at the back door when Caroline reached the top of the stairs. The knocking had ceased, but as she stepped into the kitchen, Caroline noticed a shadowy figure disappearing toward the lake. It looked like a woman.

"Should I go after her?" she asked Princess. Caroline glanced at her watch—6:00. No, whoever it was, if they'd been desperate enough, they would have stayed.

Caroline double-checked the locks on the doors and windows. She couldn't be too careful. Back in the kitchen, she glanced out the window again. No sign of anyone. "Maybe I imagined it," she mumbled. She fixed a sandwich, made a large mug of tea, and headed back to her room. "Should we just curl up with a good book, Princess?" Princess jumped on the bed and began to purr.

Dismissing the thought of reading, Caroline pulled her scrapbook out again. She had read these articles numerous times. What was it that everyone was missing? What was the common thread—besides all having disappeared from the Lake District? She skimmed over her notes: all the girls were blond, in their early 20's, athletic, vacationers camping alone or with one or two friends—females, as well.

Traci had last been seen going for a jog along the highway; Jordan, hiking up the trail behind the Smokey Campground; Karen doing early morning laps in Lake Munro, which was right next to the lake where Caroline's cottage was. In fact, all the girls had disappeared in proximity to where she was; however, and this suddenly dawned on Caroline, they were all last seen on the other side of the lake—on *his* side!

Caroline snapped the book shut. It had to be Mr. Malcolm. She'd noticed the way he looked at her when he was visiting with her dad. And the way he was always telling her to be so careful in the woods—not to go out alone—but the way he said it had always sent shivers up and down her spine. And, he was always going off to that clearing by the swamp. Sometimes her dad went with him, which Caroline didn't like. She also didn't like the way her dad behaved when he was around Mr. Malcolm—worse than his usual arrogant behaviour.

The phone startled Caroline out of her musing. She let it ring five times before answering. "Hello."

"Hi, Caroline," her mother's cheery voice came across the line. "How are you doing, honey?"

"Fine."

"Are you eating properly?"

"Yes, Mother, you've only been gone one night!"

"I know…I just worry about you."

"Don't...I'm a big girl." Caroline hadn't meant to be quite so harsh.

Her mother paused before speaking again. "Your father is coming up on Friday night to see..."

"Why?" Caroline butt in.

"He needs to see Mr. Malcolm, for some unfinished business, is what he told me."

Caroline panicked. "Is he coming to the cottage first?" she managed to ask.

"I believe that was his plan."

More silence. "Well, I guess I'll let you go; just thought you would like to know your father was coming. Love you, Caroline."

"Yep," Caroline answered mechanically as she dropped the receiver into its cradle. "He's going to ruin everything, Princess," she said, scratching the cat behind her ears. Princess looked up with disdain at having been disturbed. "Well, I'll just have to make the most of the next couple days before Dad gets here."

Caroline decided she would check her traps before dawn. She settled under her covers and attempted sleep. But it was an uneasy one—the same dream kept disturbing her peace—a faceless man was peering into her window, and he was laughing and pointing his finger at her. Then he would curl it in a beckoning motion, and the laughter would increase in its evil intonation! She turned and tossed, and tossed and turned…

The alarm buzzed loudly. Caroline reached over and hit the button. She didn't want to get up. She was so tired, and her throat hurt even worse than yesterday. But she had no choice; her father was coming, and she needed to deal with this matter before he arrived. She dressed and went downstairs. Princess was nowhere to be seen.

Caroline brewed a pot of tea and poured some into a thermos to take with her. Still, no Princess. That was exceedingly strange. She shrugged her shoulders and grabbed her jacket, a heavier one than she had worn the previous day. It was still quite foggy out, especially over the lake. Just as she was about to leave, Caroline heard a crash coming from the living room.

"Is that you, Princess?"

Silence.

Caroline grabbed a butcher knife from the drawer and then slunk toward the living room. She noticed a shadow in the far corner, sitting in her father's rocker.

"What are you doing here?" she demanded. "Show your face!"

"Hello, Caroline," the voice was vaguely familiar.

"Mr. Malcolm?" Caroline held up the knife.

"There's no need for the knife, Caroline," he said, standing and stepping out of the shadows. "I noticed someone skulking around your cottage earlier, so I came over to make sure you were okay."

"You lie!" Caroline spit out. "My doors and windows are all locked—how did you get in?"

Mr. Malcolm pointed: "That window was open."

Caroline looked. Impossible! She had secured everything! She pointed the knife menacingly. "Don't come any closer," she threatened.

"Caroline, please; I am just looking out for you as your father asked me to do. Put the knife down; we don't want anybody to get hurt here." He stepped forward.

"Not another step!" Caroline was trying to think—what would *Ruth* do? This hadn't been part of the story. Something inside her snapped and she lunged forward, planting the knife into Mr. Malcolm's abdomen. The look of shock on his face brought a smile to hers. Down he slumped, grasping at his belly. Caroline stared at him. The last thing he saw, before closing his eyes, was her smile.

Caroline sat down in her dad's chair. Things had happened too fast and she needed time to think. Her fingers tapped on the wooden arms. Well, *Ruth* already had the victim in the *room*—so, all she needed to do was get Mr. Malcolm down there. She'd have to drag him. Caroline noticed the old blanket—the one her mother loved—on the couch. Retrieving it, she laid it down and then rolled Mr. Malcolm onto it and began to pull. "Better to clean the blood from one blanket than have to clean an entire floor, hallway, and stairs," she mumbled.

Mr. Malcolm was not as heavy as Caroline thought he would be, but it still took some manoeuvring for her to get him down the basement stairs and into the room. She leaned over and checked for a pulse—it was faint. She shrugged, turned and left; some things needed to be tended to.

Caroline headed down to the dock where her canoe was tied. She noticed Mr. Malcolm's boat on the other side. Quickly, she guided it around and tied it to the stern of her canoe. When she got to the other side of the lake, she'd tie his boat to his dock, in its usual spot, retrieve her traps and then head back to the cottage and deal with him. There were a lot of questions he would need to answer—if he regained consciousness.

Mr. Malcolm opened his eyes. His entire body ached. He gazed at his surroundings. A smidgen of early morning light was filtering through the small window opposite to where he was laying. He tried to sit up, but his head was too woozy and he was hit with a sharp pain in his gut. It was then he remembered!

Caroline had stabbed him. Gerry had mentioned he thought his daughter was still not quite right from the breakdown, and he hadn't been too sure about leaving her alone up here. But to go to this extent? She had no idea what danger she could be in.

Malcolm, an undercover cop, had been staking out a house on the other side of the swamp and was getting ready to make a move now that there was some concrete proof. When the most recent girl, Cindy, had disappeared, there had been a clue left behind—something they'd never had previously—something they had not released to the media.

Another pain shot through his abdomen. "Help!" he moaned before slipping into unconsciousness again, but not before he thought he heard a cat meowing outside the door.

After securing Mr. Malcolm's boat to his dock, Caroline made her way to the pathway that led to the swamp. She had a visual picture of where she'd laid all the traps and hoped some innocent creature hadn't happened by. That was one thing that she and *Ruth* hadn't thought of.

She picked her way carefully to the first trap, leaned over and pulled it from its hiding place. Then she moved on to the next one. With three of the traps gathered, she looked around trying to remember where the fourth one was. She knew it was closer to the chairs than the others had been. As she cautiously stepped forward, Caroline was startled by the snapping of a twig. She turned quickly, lost her balance and fell. The traps scattered. She heard another twig snap, and as she looked up someone was walking steadily toward her—someone who did not look human.

The creature was tall and appeared to be rail-thin beneath the ragged clothing. Its face was hidden behind long, straw-like hair, and shadowed by a huge sun hat. The hands that crept from the sleeves of its torn jacket resembled the claws of a bird, the nails curving toward its palms. And the stench that emanated from it…

Caroline pushed herself to her feet and began backing away. Snap!

"Well, well, what do I have here," Caroline heard before blacking out. "Not blond, but I can fix that!"

Gerry had decided to head up to the cottage early and surprise his daughter. The excuse he'd given his wife, was just that—an excuse. An eerie feeling crept through his bones when he saw the front door was ajar. He stepped into the cottage and found Princess meowing at the cellar door. When she saw him, she slipped through the door, stood on the landing, and meowed again.

"What's wrong, Princess?" Gerry asked, following her.

She padded down the steps, headed for *the room* and meowed at the steel door. Gerry opened it. “Oh my God!” he exclaimed, rushing to his friend. He checked for a pulse—faint.

Gerry raced upstairs and called 911.

Caroline awoke in a strange room. Her ankle was throbbing. The door swung open, and a woman walked in. “Ah, you are awake!”

“Who are you?” Caroline managed.

“That’s not important; I need to do something about this colour,” she crooned, running her fingers through Caroline’s hair.

Caroline tried to pull away, but the woman grasped hold of her face and peered into her eyes. “There is no use, dear; there is no way out of here.”

Caroline fainted. The woman picked her up and carried her into a bathroom. “It is time to go blond—like the rest of them.”

Before the ambulance took Mr. Malcolm away, he’d managed to regain consciousness long enough to tell Gerry that it was Caroline who had stabbed him, and he had no idea where she was now.

Gerry’s decision to come up early to help Caroline close the cottage and bring her home had been a lucky one for Malcolm. He had changed his mind about letting his daughter remain by herself for five weeks, having second thoughts that she would be able to handle so much alone time. He had a gut feeling that she wasn’t fully out of the woods from her breakdown. And, according to his wife, their daughter had been behaving strangely lately—but to stab someone? Gerry glanced at the lake and noticed Princess sitting at the water's edge, staring across to Mr. Malcolm's cottage.

"You know where Caroline is?" he asked, going up to her. She rubbed around his legs, and then returned to her vigil. It was then Gerry remembered a recent conversation with his friend while they were sitting by the swamp…

"We've had that house under surveillance all summer," he'd begun, pointing to a place on the other side of the swamp. "Some woman, who used to be a top model, bought it a few years ago. Bit of a recluse. Story is that she was in a terrible fire—ended her career. One of our officers thought he saw something suspicious over there a few months ago, so we set up surveillance…"

Gerry put two and two together and called the police.

Caroline was sitting at a table in a room with mirrored walls. Six young, blond women were staring at her. "Welcome," they said in unison. Caroline recognized them all; they were the girls in the news clippings.

The *swamp woman* entered the room, followed by a young man who was pushing a cart with a movie projector on it. He pulled down a movie screen. *She* flicked on the projector. The girls turned, robotically, to watch.

Caroline saw a beautiful young woman parading on a runway. Suddenly, flames shot across the screen and out of the flames came a distinctly different woman—at least, that is how it appeared! Caroline gasped. The others just sat there, pokerfaced. *The woman* laughed hysterically.

When the film finished, the young man served supper. The girls ate mechanically. What's wrong with them? Caroline wondered. She decided not to eat, fearing the food may be drugged.

The woman noticed, came up to her and cooed gently in her ear: "It would be better for you if you eat." Caroline picked up her fork.

When the meal was finished, the girls stood in unison, and walked, single file, out of the room like a parade of models. The woman pushed Caroline into line.

The police met Gerry at the swamp's edge. "We'll have to go in quietly," said one officer. "We don't want to spook this woman."

"Are the girls still alive?" Gerry asked.

"Not sure."

Sophie and her son watched the boats crossing the swamp. They would not take her alive—or the girls. "You know what to do, Jason."

"Yes, Mommy."

After saturating the floors with gasoline, Jason flicked a lit match onto the floor and walked out the back door, disappearing into the woods. Caroline was watching from her window. She heard the hysterical laughter above her and smelled the smoke. "Help," she hollered as she tried to open her door. It was locked!

The police pushed into the burning house, rushing toward the cries for help. A woman was laughing, but they couldn't find her—the laughter soon ceased.

While waiting for the air ambulance, Gerry held his daughter's hand. "Caroline…"

Her eyes were glazed. "Who?"

"Caroline, it's okay, honey, all the girls are out. Everyone is accounted for except the woman, Sophie. It looks as though she was trying to live the life she'd lost, by collecting beautiful young women."

"There was a young man in the house; did you find him, sir?"

Gerry was puzzled that his daughter had called him sir. "No, there was no one else in the house, Caroline." Gerry gazed into his daughter's eyes and observed the return of her former illness.

After the doctors had checked Caroline's vitals and confirmed that physically she was okay, they said her mental condition would probably pass with time—she was obviously still in shock.

Gerry and Caroline were given a ride back to the cottage. Gerry put his arm around his daughter and the two of them stood gazing around at the peaceful setting. Had Gerry taken closer note of his daughter, he would have seen her staring at nothing.

Finally, "Well, Caroline, how say we lock this place up and head home?"

Caroline didn't say anything.

Gerry led her up the steps of the cottage and once inside he directed her to the couch. "Wait here while I shut things down; it won't take long."

Princess showed up out of nowhere and joined Caroline on the couch. Caroline began stroking the cat, still saying nothing, still looking at nothing. Gerry heaved a heavy sigh and left the room to finalize the closing of the cottage.

Once all the windows were locked, the blinds drawn down, the water turned off, and the furnace turned down to a minimum so the place wouldn't freeze, Gerry returned to the living room. Caroline was still sitting in the same spot, still stroking her cat.

"Do you want me to gather your things, or would you like to get them?" he asked.

For the first time since the rescue, Caroline showed a flicker of life. Without a word, she pushed Princess from her lap and headed upstairs, a silent indication she would pack her own belongings. A half an hour later, she reappeared with a suitcase and her laptop.

"Here, let me get that for you, love," Gerry said, taking the suitcase from his daughter's hand. He reached for the laptop, as well, but Caroline clutched it tightly and moved away from her father. He didn't push the issue and headed out to the car.

Caroline and Princess followed him. He opened the car trunk and placed the suitcase inside. "Would you like to put the laptop here, too?" he asked, turning to Caroline.

Without answering, Caroline opened the back door of the car and slipped inside, her laptop clutched securely in her arms. Princess jumped in after her.

Gerry sighed again. His heart was heavy. He hoped this situation would not last long, that his daughter's experience would not throw her too deeply back into the dark abyss she'd just recovered from. "I'll just be a few minutes: I have to lock the cottage," he said as he closed the car door.

Back in the cottage, Gerry looked around. This place was supposed to have been his daughter's salvation, and it appeared to have been over the past five years. But now? He made a decision, and headed for the phone and placed a call to a local realtor. Gerry told the realtor that he would leave a key under the welcome mat and asked that any paperwork be faxed to his work. Finally, taking one last scan, Gerry closed and locked the door. Until it sold, the cottage would remain closed.

As they drove slowly away from their summer home, Caroline sat in the back seat, humming and rocking back and forth. Her laptop was still clutched to her chest. Princess lay asleep beside her.

"We'll be home soon, Caroline," her father said, taking a quick glance at his daughter.

"Why do you keep calling me Caroline, sir? My name is *Ruth*."

Return to the Cottage

Caroline pulled the car to a stop by the boat house. It had been five years since the incident, since her second breakdown. Despite what the paramedics had initially thought—that she was just in shock—Caroline did not recover quickly from her ordeal at the model's house. She had spent two years in and out of institutions, but for the past three years, life had begun to steadily improve. Caroline only saw her psychiatrist, Martha, once a month now, and most of their conversations were just idle chit-chat. Caroline had decided she really had no further need of Martha's sessions at one hundred dollars an hour, so on her last visit, she'd told Martha she was going away and would not be returning anytime soon.

She had begun writing again, and this made Caroline think about the cottage on the lake. She was twenty-four now, and technically on her own; her parents were living their dream, and would be travelling the world for a couple of years. However, they had left a substantial trust fund for Caroline to live on. She'd wondered if the cottage was still owned by the couple her father had sold it to—and if it still was, would they be willing to sell. Caroline figured she could borrow a down payment from her trust fund.

After mulling the thought over for several days, Caroline had made a phone call to a realtor in the area where the cottage was. To Caroline's surprise, it was for sale again. The real estate agent, Mark, had been more than happy to make a deal, saying that that cottage had been on the market for three years and the owners would be only too pleased to get rid of it—they weren't using it. Caroline had purchased it for less than her father had sold it for five years ago.

Princess meowed from her cage. Caroline reached over and undid the latch. "We're home, baby." Princess crawled out. Caroline shut the motor off and opened her door. She stepped out of the car and breathed in the fresh northern air. Princess jumped down beside her, rubbing around Caroline's legs.

Caroline stooped over, scooped up her cat and walked up to the cottage. She would get her clothes later; she was anxious to check out her old room. The key Mark had mailed to her was a bit stiff, and she had to wiggle it in the lock before it caught hold. The door squeaked open, making an arc of dust on the floor. Caroline noticed the dust-laden sheets covering the furniture.

She wandered through the living room and into the kitchen, checking the cupboards. They were still full of dishes. She would have to take a trip to town to stock up on groceries, though. Caroline left the kitchen and headed for the stairs and her old room. She opened the door. "Strange," she murmured. The furniture that had been there five years ago was still in place. Princess darted in and jumped up on the desk.

There was one more place to check out before bringing in her luggage—the basement. Back on the main floor, Caroline tried to open the basement door. It was locked. She looked around for a key, but could not see one. "I'll have to call the realtor," she said to Princess.

Princess meowed.

Caroline stepped onto the porch and noticed the Muskoka chairs were still there—just a bit more weather-worn than they had been five years ago. They still faced Mr. Malcolm's place across the lake. She wondered if he still owned it. He had recovered from the wound she had inflicted on him, but she had not really cared to know anything more about him. Even though he had turned out to be a cop, he still gave her the creeps. "I'll bet my bottom dollar that he's a dirty cop," Caroline said to Princess.

The cat meowed and rubbed around her legs. "Okay, I'll go get the luggage, and your food!" she laughed.

After unpacking her suitcases, Caroline went outside to sit on the porch, taking a glass of white wine with her. She twirled the glass in her hand. Princess sat in the other chair. Suddenly, she noticed a movement on the porch across the lake. Could it be Mr. Malcolm? No, whoever it was moved with a youthful grace. The person noticed her looking his way and waved. She grimaced and waved back. Maybe she would take the canoe across tomorrow and see who it was. It was good to know your neighbours. Hopefully, there was still a canoe in the boathouse.

Caroline headed back into the cottage, locked the door and as she drew the curtains, she noticed the man was still gazing her way. She reached for the wine bottle, refilled her glass and headed up the stairs to her room. She had left her laptop on and the screen saver was flipping through its pictures. Caroline moved the mouse and a word document appeared on the screen. She glanced over the first few paragraphs and then shut the file down. "Not today, *Ruth,* it's too late and I am bushed."

Caroline stretched out on her bed and lay quietly for a few minutes. Princess jumped up and began kneading in the pillow behind her head. The cat's purring lulled Caroline to sleep.

The morning awoke in anger. Black clouds had rolled in overnight, covering the area with murky darkness. A thick fog hung over the lake. Caroline had slept better than usual, but not well enough to not have the dream. And this time, there were two new faces in the kaleidoscope—faces faintly familiar to her, but from where?

She splashed water on her face and headed downstairs. Princess trotted after her, almost tripping her on the staircase. "I have to go into town to get some supplies; you stay here and keep an eye on things," Caroline said, putting food in the cat's dish. "I might be a while because I want to stop by the realtor and pick up a key for the basement door."

Princess didn't respond. She was busy eating. Caroline grabbed her keys and headed out. She glanced across the lake but the fog was so dense she could not see Mr. Malcolm's cottage. She wondered if the stranger was watching. She wondered who he was.

After buying her groceries, Caroline stopped at the realtor. "I need a key to the basement door," she said to Sally, the secretary.

"Mr. Dawson is showing a house right now; I'll leave him a note and have him give you a call if there is one."

"How long do you think Mark will be?" Caroline queried.

Sally's eyebrows rose at Caroline's use of her boss's first name. "Well, he left about an hour ago…"

"So he should be back soon then?" Caroline interrupted. "Why don't you page him and let him know I'm here; I can wait. Save us both a trip." Caroline smiled.

Sally hesitated before picking up the phone. "Well, I guess if you want to wait…hello, Mr. Dawson. Caroline is here wondering about a key to the basement door in her cottage…you gave her all the keys…okay, I'll tell her…yes…you're going for lunch now…okay, see you at 1:00…no, no other calls…bye."

She put the phone down and turned to Caroline. "Mr. Dawson does not have a key. He suggested you call a locksmith and get a new one made. He recommends Mr. Calvin. I'll give you his number." Sally paused, as though she wanted to say something else. Finally, "Why would anyone put a lock on a basement door on the inside of a house?"

"I have no idea," Caroline answered evasively.

"Oh well, here is Mr. Calvin's number and address. His office is actually a couple of streets over if you want to stop by there. You might catch him on his lunch break."

Caroline took the piece of paper. "Thank you." She turned and left. She was a bit disappointed at not having seen Mark again—he intrigued her. As she headed out the door, she thought back to the first time she had met Mark in person. There had been something familiar about him, but she had not been able to quite put her finger on what it was.

The locksmith's shop was easy to find and Caroline was lucky to catch him just as he was leaving. "Mr. Calvin," Caroline called out. "A moment of your time please."

"How might I help you, miss?" He stopped at his truck door.

"Mr. Dawson from the real estate office gave me your name. He said you could make me a new lock for my basement door. Apparently, the original key has been lost. How soon do you think you could come out to the cottage?"

"Let me check my schedule book," he said, opening the truck door and reaching inside. He flipped through some pages. "Hmmm…I could come out at 9:00 tomorrow morning. Which cottage is it?"

"I'm at 55 Deerfoot Lane."

"Deerfoot Lane…55…something familiar about that address…I know the place…oh yeah, some city folks used to own it…when they sold, I installed the new locks for the folks that bought the cottage—they didn't stay long, though. Place has been empty for quite some time now."

Caroline did not want to let this man know that she was quite familiar with the cottage. The past was something she did not wish to discuss with a stranger. "Nine o'clock will be fine;

I'll see you then. Sorry, but I do have to run now. Thank you, Mr. Calvin." Caroline turned quickly and headed back to her car.

The sun had finally broken through the clouds and the fog had lifted, making the drive back to the cottage more pleasant. Caroline took in the surrounding scenery. Not too much had changed in five years. There was a new cottage being built, though, just before she turned onto Deerfoot Lane. Caroline wondered who her new neighbour was going to be.

Caroline glanced across the lake before getting out of her car. All appeared quiet. She grabbed her grocery bags. An agitated Princess greeted her at the front door.

"Come on now, I wasn't gone that long." Caroline walked into the kitchen and glanced up at the clock. It was 1:15, later than she'd thought. Her stomach grumbled. She rummaged through the groceries and pulled out a package of fig cookies. Princess ran to her dish.

"Nothing for you until supper; people eat three times a day, not overweight cats!"

Princess flattened her ears and switched her tail angrily. Finally, in a huff, she left. Caroline heard her running up the stairs.

After putting her groceries away, Caroline made a cup of tea and headed out to the porch. It was still too early for wine. She could see Mr. Malcolm's cottage quite clearly. It appeared deserted. She glanced down the shoreline and noticed that the new cottage at the end of Deerfoot Lane was actually not far from Mr. Malcolm's. She noted where the construction of a boat house and dock had already begun. Whoever had bought that piece of land must have enough money to build everything at once. Most cottagers in the area did things in stages.

Suddenly a figure stepped out of the woods and walked down to the half-built dock. Even though there was something familiar about the person, Caroline could not tell who it was because she didn't have a clear view of his face. He turned and looked over toward her cottage, but his hat was shadowing his face and she still couldn't get a good look at him.

Mr. Calvin showed up promptly at 9:00 the next morning. Caroline was in an unusually indifferent mood. She had polished off a bottle of wine the previous evening and had not slept well. The dream had repeated itself, but the faces were still hidden.

"Previous owner installed this. I guess they were a bit nervous about what had happened in the basement," Mr. Calvin commented as he got started.

Caroline sat down at her table and watched him. "Do you know who owns the new cottage at the beginning of Deerfoot Lane?" she asked.

Mr. Calvin looked up. There was a puzzled expression on his face. "Why the real estate fellow, Mark Dawson; didn't he mention that you and he would be neighbours?"

Caroline glanced out her window. "No…no, he failed to mention that. How long has he been around these parts?"

"A couple of years. No one really knows where he came from. Just showed up one day. Went into partnership with Mr. Donaldson, who owned the real estate office. Strange thing happened, though: Donaldson, who had never been sick a day in his life, suddenly took ill. Died about six months after Mark went into business with him. Course he was old, and I hear that sometimes that happens to folks. Mark's done a good job though…there, that should do it. Here're your new keys." He paused. "Want me to take a look down there for you? If it's been locked up, you never know what might be there."

"No, it's okay, thanks; how much do I owe you?"

"Well if it's cash we can forgo the taxes; sixty should cover it."

Caroline went to get her purse. When she returned, she handed Mr. Calvin the money. He looked at her for a moment and then said: "You be careful now. There have been some strange things going on around here lately."

"Like what?"

"Well, I don't really want to say too much…" he paused. "You're the girl that lived here back when that crazy model was kidnapping all those girls, aren't you?" Mr. Calvin raised his eyebrows questioningly.

"Your point being?" Caroline didn't feel comfortable with this line of questioning. Her past was her business.

When she didn't answer him, he continued: "That cop you stabbed…now don't take me wrong…he said you were mighty scared…said he shouldn't have been in the house like that…said he never really blamed you and that he was just glad your dad came along when he did, or he would have been a goner. Well, he rented his cottage out for a few years; he just returned this past summer. His grandson is with him. Troubled boy if you ask me. I was out there to change the locks because Mr. Malcolm wasn't sure if any of the renters had kept a key and he wasn't willing to take any chances, being a retired cop and all. He retired after the incident, you know.

"Well, I met the grandson; looks a lot like his grandpa, but there was something about him that I didn't cotton to. There was a real angry look in his eyes, which were an icy-grey colour. He watched every move I made, extremely uncomfortable feeling." Mr. Calvin paused for breath.

Caroline did not want to hear any more. "Well, that is good to know, Mr. Calvin; I will be sure to be very careful. Is Mr. Malcolm there with his grandson?"

"Yep. Heard the boy's parents needed a break from him and that the old man offered to straighten him out."

"I see."

"Well, can't believe everything you hear; some of it could just be idle gossip. Only wanted to warn you to be careful."

Caroline smiled. "One can never be too careful nowadays, even in a paradise like this." She began walking toward the front door to give Mr. Calvin the hint that he needed to move along. He had not actually told her what strange things were going on, but she did not care to know at this point in time. "You have a good day now, Mr. Calvin," she said as she opened the door for him. "And thanks for your concern; I'll be sure to be careful," she repeated.

"You do that, Caroline," he smiled and then paused on the porch as though he were going to say something more. Caroline did not give him a chance. She shut the door. From her window, she watched him leave. When his dust had settled, she headed for the kitchen and the basement door. Princess was sitting beside it, ready to follow her mistress anywhere she was going.

The basement smelled stale. Thick layers of dust were everywhere. "Lot of cleaning up to do down here," Caroline muttered. She passed by the wall with the traps, surprised they were still there; someone must have found them by the swamp and returned them to the cottage. She wandered down to the room. She stepped inside and shivered. There was still a faint red spot on the floor where Mr. Malcolm had lain. Caroline glanced up at the window—still barred. The sun filtered through and she followed the dancing dust particles to a corner and noticed a pile of boxes.

"I wonder what's in these?" she said to Princess. Caroline brushed the dust off and opened the top box. Inside, to her surprise, was her scrapbook that she had kept under her bed. "I wonder why the new owners didn't just throw this out."

She pulled out the book and began flipping through the pages. Old memories started to pour into her head. She read and re-read the news clippings and went over her notes. The final article was not glued in. It had obviously been put there by someone else for it was the news story of the rescue. A picture of each one of the girls, including hers, was spread across the top of the story. A report given by Mr. Malcolm was in another clipping. It was dated a couple days after the main article, obviously because he had not been well enough to give a statement on the day of the take-down. There was a picture of the model, taken before the fire that had disfigured her, and a short story about the tragedy that had led to her kidnapping the girls. Caroline tucked the book under her arm and headed upstairs.

She set the scrapbook on the table, made herself a cup of tea, and then sat down to re-read the articles she had only scanned through. Mr. Malcolm was saying how he didn't blame his friend's daughter for stabbing him and he was sorry he had broken into the cottage the way he had. He thanked the cat for showing Caroline's father where he was—he actually owed his life to the cat. It went on about the surveillance and other details.

There was one thing that really bothered Caroline, though. Not one of the statements made by the other girls who had been in that house mentioned anything about the woman's son. "Was I the only one who saw you?" Caroline leaned back in her chair and put her hands behind her head. Princess jumped up on the table and settled on one of the news clippings.

Mark Dawson was ready to call it a day, but he was getting fed up with the contractors delaying the completion of his cottage. He was anxious to move in, especially now that she was there. She certainly was a looker. He picked up his phone and dialled the contractor's number.

"Wesley's Construction, how may I help you?"

"Wesley there?"

"He's in a meeting right now; may I take a message?"

"Get him out of his meeting; I want to talk to him right now!"

"I'm afraid he left explicit instructions not to be disturbed, Mr., ah…"

"Dawson. He told me my cottage would be finished by now, but it seems nowhere near completion. I want to speak to him now!" Mark's voice rose angrily. The phone went on hold. He tapped his pen on the desk.

Finally, "Hey there, Mark, sorry about that. I realize we are behind schedule a bit…"

"Not a bit, Wesley, a whole lot. I need the cottage finished by the end of the month; I'm tired of living in the upstairs of that boarding house! You get your men out there tomorrow morning."

"That's a pretty tall order, Mark."

"Well, you'll be short on the next payment if you don't get it done!" Mark slammed the receiver down.

Wesley stared at the phone. There was something strange about Mark Dawson, something he could not put his finger on. The man didn't look him straight in the eye—something Wesley had first noticed about him. And then there was the mysterious, untimely death of Mr. Donaldson, and how conveniently Mark had taken over the business. He picked up the phone and called his building foreman.

Caroline was working on her story when she heard the whistling. She walked over to her window and was just in time to catch a glimpse of someone stepping up onto her porch. Quickly, she shut off her computer and headed downstairs. She opened the front door just as the young man was about to ring the bell. He jumped back, startled.

"May I help you?" Caroline asked.

"I…I…live across the lake there," he pointed. "Noticed we had a new neighbour so thought to come across and introduce myself." He stuck his hand out: "Nathan."

Caroline did not take his proffered hand. He was scraggly looking, and it appeared as though he'd slept in his clothes. Nathan shoved his hand into his jeans' pocket and shuffled his feet. He was wearing a worn-out pair of sneakers. "Well, I guess I must have caught you at a bad time," he said and began to turn away.

Caroline reconsidered her position. Maybe Nathan could tell her what his grandfather was up to. "I'm sorry for my rudeness—please, have a seat," she motioned to the Muskoka chairs. "Would you like a drink? I have some pop in the fridge—or wine if you'd prefer."

"Pop would be nice. I'm too young to legally drink," he grinned, putting an emphasis on the word, legally.

"You look old enough," Caroline stated, her way of finding out Nathan's age.

"Only sixteen."

Caroline headed into the cottage and returned a few minutes later with two pops. "How is your grandfather doing?" she asked.

Nathan looked up at her. Yes, his eyes were an icy grey, just like Mr. Calvin had described, but Caroline did not see them as angry eyes—they had more of a vacant look to them. "He's okay," Nathan finally answered. "Miserable as ever, though; something has gotten under his skin. I think it has to do with those two girls they found."

Caroline sat up at attention. She swallowed hard. "What two girls?"

"Well, they were found in the woods just down from my grandfather's cottage. He said they hadn't been killed at the same time; looked to have been about a week apart. What really got to my grandfather was that they were both blond and their faces had been severely burned."

Caroline dropped her drink. Were these the mysterious events Mr. Calvin had been going to tell her about? Her father had told her the model had not made it out of the house alive, yet the similarity of these two new victims was uncanny. Then again, she had not killed her victims, only kidnapped and drugged them.

Nathan was handing her the dropped tin of pop. "I didn't mean to scare you, miss…you didn't really tell me your name," he added.

"Caroline." Her voice was husky with emotion. "I heard your grandfather retired from the police force?" she added.

"Yeah, he did, but they call him in for special cases. He told me that he worked a similar set of circumstances a few years ago." Nathan paused. "How did you know he was a cop?

"He was a friend of my dad, who used to own this cottage." Caroline looked away. "I think you better go now. Please don't tell your grandfather you met me."

Nathan looked puzzled.

"I am the girl that stabbed him."

"Oh my God!" Nathan lifted his hand to his mouth.

"He'd probably prefer not to know I am living here."

It was at that point Caroline noticed a change in Nathan's eyes. They looked angry, almost evil. "Mum's the word,

Caroline. I don't get along all that well with him anyway." He got up and walked down the steps, and then turned back to her. "He usually leaves early in the morning and doesn't come back until after dark. Come over anytime. I get lonely." He smiled.

Caroline definitely saw a flicker of evil cross over his face then.

Caroline was pacing in the kitchen. Her nerves were tight. Princess knew enough not to bother her when she was in this mood. "What would *Ruth* do?" Caroline asked the cat. The phone rang.

"Hello."

"Hi, is this Caroline?"

"Yes, who is this?"

"Mark."

"Oh, hello Mark, who was too busy to come and help me out yesterday."

"I am really sorry about that; I truly was tied up with a client and to close the deal I had to take him out to lunch. Mr. Calvin looked after you, though, didn't he?"

"Yes. He was very informative too. He sure knows a lot about what is going on around here." Caroline paused for effect. "Mentioned you own the new cottage at the beginning of Deerfoot Lane; I wonder why you didn't say that when I bought this place."

"Actually, I was going to surprise you…"

"And just how were you going to do that, and when?" Caroline spit sarcastically. "And why?" she added.

"Well, I was going to ask you out for supper on Saturday night and then when I drove you home I was going to stop by the cottage and show it to you. The contractors have been messing around and are way behind schedule, but I think they might step it up now, especially after our little talk this morning."

"I see."

"So, is it a date?"

Caroline thought for a moment. He was a good-looking man, even though there was something strangely familiar and disconcerting about him. It would not hurt to spend a pleasant evening with someone of the opposite sex; after all, it had been a while. "Sure," she finally answered. "What time shall I be ready?"

"How's six?"

"Okay."

No sooner had Caroline hung up the phone, it rang again. "Hello."

"Hi, Caroline, sorry to bother you; I believe I left one of my tools at the top of the stairs just inside your basement door. Do you think I could swing by and pick it up? You can put it on the porch if you like so I won't have to bother you."

"I'll do that, Mr. Calvin."

Caroline opened the basement door. There on the top stair was a small file. Funny she had not noticed it before. She took the file to the front porch and set it on the top stair. She looked across the lake and detected Nathan looking back at her. He waved. Caroline turned quickly and went into the cottage, shutting and locking the door. She had had enough company for one day.

Caroline threw a T.V. dinner in the microwave and poured a glass of wine while she was waiting for her meal to finish cooking. Princess was nowhere to be seen at the moment. "Probably upstairs, asleep on my bed," Caroline mumbled. When the dinner was finished, she took it up to her room and sat down at her computer. Just as she had thought, Princess was on the bed.

"Well, *Ruth*, what say you about this turn of events today?" Caroline turned the computer on and went into her story––a story she had started five years ago, but hadn't finished. She leaned back for a moment, thinking. And then, she began to type…

Ruth had stumbled across the bodies in the woods just down from Mr. M.'s place. Why had the police let him out? Oh yeah, not enough evidence, it said in the paper. She took out her cell phone and called 911, and then waited by the bodies until the police came. She did not like the fact that both the girls appeared to have been blond, although, with the one it was hard to tell, her entire head had been burned so badly. It also appeared that they had not died at the same time, one being more decomposed than the other…

Caroline wrote feverishly for another two hours; her fingers flying over the keys as though they were possessed. Finally, she pushed her chair back from the desk and went downstairs. Princess followed her and ran to her dish. Caroline filled it with kibble and then poured herself another glass of wine. She walked over to the window, which faced the lake, and peered over to Mr. Malcolm's cottage. There was a light beaming on the front porch, but the inside of the cottage was in darkness. Just as she was about to turn away, she noticed a moving shadow on the lake. She tried to focus. The shadow was headed in the direction of her cottage. For sure it was a boat, but she could not tell whether there were one or two people in it.

Caroline walked around each room and made sure all the doors and windows were locked. Who would be out on the lake at this time of night? Only a fool would dare, especially without a light to guide their way. The lake was known for rocks and was dangerous in the best of light. She looked around nervously, poured another glass of wine and headed up to her room. It was most likely nothing to worry about—probably just some new, fool cottager that was unaware of the perils in the lake. Well, they would learn soon enough if they hit one of those rocks!

After turning her computer off, Caroline turned her television on, fluffed the pillows on her bed, and then pulled her comforter up to waist level. She rested her head on the headboard. The ten o'clock news would be starting soon. She sipped on her wine. Princess lay curled on the end of the bed. There was a quiet pause between programs…and then…

"What was that Princess? Did you hear that?" Caroline jumped out of bed and went to the window. Pulling the curtain across, she gazed out at the lake. "Did you hear that scream?"

Princess flicked her ears and went back to sleep. Her tail swished a couple of times to show her mistress she was not pleased with having been rudely awakened. Caroline let the curtain drop and crawled back into bed. The news came on. "Probably nothing. I guess I am just jittery with everything going on around here, eh?"

"Another body was found today. Once again the police will have to wait for forensics to identify the young woman as the face was severely burned. Like the other two, this woman was blond. The body was found by a local police officer who lives on the lake...the body looks to have been there for about three days...

Caroline turned the television off and buried herself deeper under the covers. Sleep finally overtook her, even though it was a restless one.

Five o'clock found Caroline crawling from her bed. She put her housecoat on and went downstairs, looking around nervously as she entered the kitchen. "You need to get hold of yourself, girl," she whispered to the emptiness. Caroline plugged in the kettle and sat down at the table. She looked over at the calendar. It was Friday. Maybe she would take the canoe over to Mr. Malcolm's cottage and pay a visit to Nathan. Maybe she could get him to tell her more about the girl that had been found. After all, it was his grandfather who had found her!

Caroline took her cup of tea upstairs and sat down at her computer. It was too early to pay a call on anyone, so she may as well write more on her novel. "Good morning, *Ruth*," she said as the document appeared on the screen. "Whatever are we going to do now? There was another body you know—just like the others. I bet you already knew that though, didn't you?" Caroline began to type…

> *Ruth rushed up the steps of the police station. As the head crime reporter for the paper, the officer in charge was obliged to give her a statement. She went straight to his office. There was a scowl on his face as she entered.*
>
> *"I can't give you anything today, Ruth. We have to keep this under wraps; we don't want all the cottagers panicking."*
>
> *"They need to know what is going on, especially the women, especially the blond women!" Ruth emphasized.*
>
> *"We are following up on some good leads right now and we don't want to spook whoever is killing these girls. I simply cannot give you any more information. I assure you that..."*
>
> *"Yeah, yeah—I know the drill; I'll be the first to know!" Ruth leaned over the captain's*

desk. "Well, I guess I will just have to print my speculations then." She smiled.

"Ruth, you know you can't do that; be reasonable."

"I am reasonable—for a blond!" Ruth turned and stomped out of his office...

Caroline shut the computer off at 8:00, dressed for her trip across the lake, and headed downstairs. She filled Princess's bowl and then poured herself a bowl of cereal. When she was finished eating, she headed down to the boat house. Princess was watching her, nervously pacing along the windowsill.

The door to the boat house creaked open. She was happy to see the canoe was still there. She pulled a paddle off the wall and crouched down to undo the rope. It was then that Caroline saw the body!

It was Mr. Malcolm. His hands were tied behind his back and there was a red gash on his head. It looked like he had bled a great deal, by the size of the puddle of blood beneath him. "Maybe he's just knocked out," Caroline muttered as she knelt down and felt for a pulse. The body was cold. She looked around nervously. Finally, Caroline stood and headed to the cottage to call the police.

An ambulance arrived before the police. They must have placed the call because Caroline hadn't thought of calling an ambulance. She stood up from the porch step, where she had been waiting, and led the paramedics down to the boat house. Caroline showed them the body.

One of them felt for a pulse and shook his head. "Better leave the body until the police get here," he said. "They will want pictures."

A police siren broke the morning silence. The cruiser squealed to a stop at the boathouse. Two officers got out, slamming their car doors. "What do we have here?" the male officer asked. "Oh shit!" he added when he saw who was in the canoe. "Got your camera, Sarah?" He turned to Caroline. "You the one who found the body?"

"Yes."

"What time was that?"

"Shortly after 8:00. I came down to take the canoe out on the lake." Caroline thought it best not to mention she had actually been going over to Mr. Malcolm's cottage to visit his grandson.

"You live here?"

"Yes."

"Did you not hear anything during the night?" The officer's voice was harsh.

"Well, I thought I heard someone scream around 10:00 last night…"

"And you didn't think to check it out?"

"I got up and looked out my window…it was dark…I couldn't see anything…I wasn't going to go outside at that time of night, especially with all those girls that have been murdered around here."

"You didn't think to call the police? I mean you heard a scream!"

"Jason, lighten up," Sarah walked up with the camera. "She didn't kill Malcolm; she just found the body, and she found the body because she lives here." Sarah started snapping pictures of the crime scene. She turned to Caroline. "Did you touch anything?"

"Just the paddle and the side of the boat," Caroline answered. "I also felt his neck for a pulse before I called you guys."

"You may as well go up to the cottage; we'll be up to take your statement when we finish here." Sarah turned to Jason.

"Better send someone over to tell Malcolm's grandson about his grandfather. Nathan is probably still sleeping."

Jason walked over to the police car and called the precinct to send a car out to Malcolm's cottage. As Caroline passed by, she noticed the irritated look on his face. "I know who you are," he said as he stepped out of the car. "You're the girl who stabbed Malcolm five years ago. Did you come back to finish the job?"

"I don't think I have to answer that!"

"Well, you will have to later." Jason turned and walked back to the boat house.

Once inside the cottage, Caroline poured herself a glass of wine. It was early, but it had already been a long morning. This was a nightmare! She did not want to be alone, but who could she call? She did not have any friends up here. Well, there was Mark––possibly. Maybe, if he were not busy, he would come out and sit with her. And, from the way that officer had spoken to her, she just might need a lawyer. Hopefully, Mark would know a good one. She picked up the phone and dialled the real estate office.

"Dawson Realty, Sally here; how might I direct your call?"

"Is Mark in?"

"No, I am sorry, Mr. Dawson isn't in. He phoned earlier and said he would be out of town this morning. I don't expect him until early afternoon. Would you like to leave a message?"

"Tell him Caroline called." Caroline shut the phone off and then downed her glass of wine. She walked over to the window and peered down at the boat house. The paramedics were lifting Mr. Malcolm's body onto a gurney. She glanced across the lake. Nathan was sitting on his porch, watching. Caroline let the curtain drop back into place.

"What are we going to do now, *Ruth*? It looks like that officer has it in for me. What are we going to do about him?"

There was a tap on the door and the police walked in. "Where would you like us to sit?" Sarah asked.

Caroline motioned to the living room chairs. "Here is as good as anywhere; would either of you like some tea? I have a pot on."

"Coffee for me," Jason answered.

"I don't have coffee," Caroline grinned at the thought of not giving Jason what he wanted. She did not like him any more than she had liked Mr. Malcolm.

Jason drilled Caroline with numerous questions. He had a gut feeling Caroline had killed Malcolm. He had read the file on her from five years ago as soon as he had found out she was the one who had bought the cottage. He had warned Malcolm about her, but Malcolm had just fluffed it off and told him that she had just been a kid then; there was nothing to worry about. Now he was dead; found in her boathouse, by her.

After an hour of questions, Caroline stood. "You know, I don't like what you are insinuating, officer. I'm not saying anything more until I have a lawyer present. If you are going to arrest me, then do it."

Jason's face turned red. He opened his mouth to say something, but before he could speak, Sarah stood. "I think that will be all for now, Caroline. We'll be in touch. Let's go, Jason." Sarah gave her partner a stern look. "We need o go talk to Nathan," she added.

Caroline saw them to the door. She watched the car speed down the lane, throwing stones everywhere in its haste. "That Officer Jason sure is ticked," she said to Princess. Caroline climbed the stairs to her room and turned on the computer. "Okay, *Ruth*; now what?" Caroline began to type…

Ruth was not happy with the turn of events.
Who did that police officer think he was, refusing

to give her the scoop on the story? After all, she had been the one who had discovered the first two bodies. Come to think of it, he had been a pain in her side ever since he had come to the Precinct and taken over Captain Joe's position. Ruth really missed Joe. She had never printed anything he told her was off the record, but he had always given her the full scoop.

She slammed her car door shut and sat for a moment before taking off for home. On the way, she had a change of mind and headed for the location where the last body had been found. Maybe she would be able to piece together some information on her own. As she approached the wooded area, she got the uneasy feeling she was being followed. Ruth checked her rearview mirror. Not a car in sight. She shut the engine off and got out of the car. Before entering the woods, she checked up and down the road again...

Caroline's train of thought was disturbed by the doorbell. She saved her document, shut the computer off, and headed downstairs. When she opened the door, Nathan was standing there. He looked angry.

"Do you know what the police are trying to say, Caroline? They think I killed my grandfather!"

Caroline was shocked. "What did you say to them?"

"Nothin'. That male cop...I can't even remember his name, I'm so upset...he was badgering me like crazy."

"Don't take it too personally; he did the same thing to me. Spent an entire hour here, drilling me about why I killed your grandfather. If I had killed him, why would I have called the police? The guy must be dense!" Caroline's statement elicited a giggle from Nathan. "Want a pop?" she offered.

"Sure."

Caroline returned with a pop for Nathan and a glass of wine for herself. She pointed him to one of the Muskoka chairs. "So, why does he think you did it?"

"There were fresh marks on the sand beside my grandfather's boat, and fresh footprints—mine, of course, because I had the boat out yesterday. I told him that, but it was like he didn't believe me."

"When did you have the boat out?"

"After supper for a bit."

"What time?" Caroline was curious now, wondering if Nathan had been the person she had seen on the lake last night.

Nathan tensed. "I don't know; after supper."

"Was it dark?"

"I don't know—yeah, maybe."

"You should know whether it was dark or not," Caroline pushed.

"What difference should it make to you? Gee-whiz, you are as bad as that cop!"

"I saw someone on the lake last night, but I couldn't tell who it was; nor could I quite see how many people were in the boat. And the boat was heading toward my cottage."

"What are you saying, Caroline?" Nathan stood. His face was contorted in anger. "Do you think I killed my grandfather and then planted him in your boat house?" He threw the pop can out onto the driveway and the liquid bubbled into the stones. "I'm out of here. I came here 'cause I thought you were my friend!"

"Nathan," Caroline reached for his arm, "I'm sorry."

"You have no idea how sorry you are going to be for this!" he retorted, and before Caroline could say another word, Nathan was running to his boat.

Princess was pawing at the screen door. Caroline opened it for her. "What have I done, kitty? I didn't mean to accuse Nathan of killing his grandfather, but so many strange things have been happening around here." She sat down on the chair. Princess jumped onto her lap. "And he was on the lake last night." The sound of a car drew her attention to the lane. She hoped it was not the police returning to drill her with more questions. If so, should she tell them Nathan had been on the lake last night after dark?

To Caroline's relief, a red convertible pulled up in front of the porch. Mark Dawson stepped out. "I came as soon as I heard," he said, bounding up the steps. "Are you okay, Caroline?"

"I'm fine," she replied.

He studied her for a moment. "You look a tad shaken." He paused and then pointed to the lake. "Who was that? He looked pretty angry."

"Nathan, Mr. Malcolm's grandson. He came here looking for a shoulder and I'm afraid what I gave him was accusations. I didn't mean to, but he said he was on the lake last night and I saw someone on the lake; I was just trying to get him to tell me what time he was out there so I could rule him out."

Mark's face lost its concern. "You saw someone on the lake last night?"

Before she thought about his question, Caroline answered. "Yes, but it was so dark I couldn't see clearly, and I actually couldn't tell if there were one or two people in the boat. I just made sure all my doors and windows were locked up and went to bed. Then, around ten o'clock I thought I heard a scream, but I wasn't going to go outside and check it out."

"So you didn't see who it might have been?"

Caroline wondered why Mark was asking that question when she had just told him she had not seen who was in the boat. His eyes were very dark, bringing back memories of someone from long ago, but she still could not put her finger on whom. "I told you, I didn't see their faces!" she retorted sharply.

"So, there was more than one then?" Mark pushed on.

"Look," Caroline shouted, "if you came over here to badger me about something that is really none of your business, you should just leave! I've had enough for one day! There was another girl found…killed the same as the other two…face severely burned. I found a dead body in my boat house this morning…the police think I killed him…I just about accused his grandson of being the killer…and now here you are pumping questions at me…what's going on with you? I thought you came over because you were concerned about me? If that is not the real reason you are here, just turn around, get back in your fancy car and leave! And you can forget about our date tomorrow night while you're at it!"

"Caroline, I'm sorry; I didn't mean…well, I don't really know what got into me. I guess I was just worried. When people get worried, sometimes things come out the wrong way. I will be living on this lake pretty soon too and I want to make sure it is safe. My mother and sister will be joining me once I get settled." Mark reached for Caroline's hand.

Princess hissed and leapt at Mark. He jumped out of the way, just in time. "What's wrong with your cat?"

"Princess!" Caroline reached down and scooped her up. "What's wrong, baby?" Princess was looking at Mark, her ears flat on her head; her tail switching angrily. "She was probably upset that you were yelling at me. You know, Mark, I thank you for coming over and all, but I think we should just call it a day and start over tomorrow. Before you go, though, could you tell me if there are any good lawyers around these parts? The way that one officer was badgering me, I think I might need one."

"I'll confer with my secretary, Sally, on who would be the best one, and have her give you a call. I truly am sorry, Caroline." Mark started down the steps. "I'll pick you up tomorrow at six if that is still okay. In the meantime, if anything else out of the ordinary happens, don't hesitate to call me. Here's my card; it has my cellphone number."

"Just have Sally call me with the lawyer's name; I'll still have to think about our date," Caroline articulated.

"No problem." Mark got in his car and drove away.

Caroline looked across the lake. Nathan was standing on his porch staring over at her cottage. She turned to go in the house. It was then that she noticed the file she had left out for Mr. Calvin was still there. Why had he not picked it up like he had said he would? Oh well, she would just leave it. He was probably busy. If he really needed it, he would be by. Caroline stepped into the cottage and locked the door.

Caroline had a difficult time sleeping again that night. Mark's face kept flitting in and out of her dreams. One moment it showed concerned; the next moment it was contorted with fury. And then Nathan's face leered up, and the next thing she saw was Nathan and Mark in a canoe, and Mr. Malcolm was tied up in the bottom. There was blood all over his face! And Nathan and Mark were laughing! And when they got to the boathouse, Mr. Calvin was waiting for them and he patted them both on the back and told them it was a job well done! He had a young, blond girl with him, a file up against her neck. There was a gas can in his hand. The girl looked terrified. And then the phone was ringing…

Princess's meowing woke Caroline up. The phone was actually ringing. She grabbed the extension by her bed. "Hello."

"You're next," a gritty voice spoke into the receiver.

"Who is this?" Caroline shouted.

The phone went dead. Caroline pushed the talk button. There was no signal. She looked over at her computer. The monitor, which she usually left on, was off. She tried the lamp by her bed. It would not turn on. Caroline felt around in the night table drawer for her emergency matches. She kept a candle in each room. She felt her way over to the desk and located her candle, lit it, and then headed downstairs to find her cellphone. "Stay here, Princess," Caroline hissed at the cat.

Once in the kitchen, Caroline located her purse and dug around for her cellphone. She turned it on and waited impatiently for the signal. Finally. She dialled 911.

"Emergency Department…how may I direct your call?"

"Police Department…hurry."

"What is the problem, miss?"

"I think someone is trying to kill me!" Caroline's voice was hysterical. "Someone called and said I was next and then my lines went dead and my hydro has been cut off and I had to find my cellphone and I need you to get a police car out here right away. I'm at 55 Deerfoot Lane."

"We'll dispatch someone as soon as possible, miss. In the meantime, make sure all your doors and windows are locked."

A loud crash came from the living room. It sounded like breaking glass. "Did you hear that?" Caroline screamed into the phone. "Someone's in my cottage!"

"Get yourself somewhere safe, miss. As I already said, an officer will be there as soon as possible. I'll stay on the line with you, so don't hang up."

Caroline darted for the basement door and ran down the steps. There was one place she might be safe. The room. As she ran past the traps, she had an idea. She could hear someone moving around upstairs and she quickened her pace.

She closed the door on the room and slunk down to the floor. Her breathing was irregular. "Oh, *Ruth*; what are we going to do?" Tears ran down Caroline's cheeks. She looked up at the barred window and thought she saw a shadow cross by.

"Have you dispatched a cruiser yet?" she whispered into the phone. "There is someone in my house. I am hiding in the basement, but it is only a matter of time before they come down here…"

"A car has been dispatched, miss. Just stay quiet; someone will be there soon."

Caroline fixed her eyes on the window. The moon cast a beam of light into the room. She moved out of its range, crouching in a corner. She could hear the footsteps upstairs. She could hear things being moved and dropped to the floor. She prayed Princess would stay hidden.

Nathan had been pretty upset at how Caroline had questioned him, but as the day wore away, he realized that she was just scared. He'd had a fight with his grandfather and he had actually decided to leave. Nathan had taken his grandfather's boat onto the lake with the intention to dump it way down the lake. But, as he had rowed away, he had second thoughts and turned back to the cottage. When he had arrived back, his grandfather was not there anymore, so he figured he had just gone into town for a drink to cool off after their fight. Of course, the next morning, he was told his grandfather had been murdered and the police were treating him as a suspect.

He had been gazing over at Caroline's cottage when he noticed some movement down by her boat house. Nathan began to worry, so headed to his boat. He paddled across the lake, pulled up on the shore just down from Caroline's and then walked in the shadows up to the cottage. He heard the window break just as he reached the back of the building. Nathan hid in the bushes next to a basement window. Finally, he gathered the courage to try and get in the house and see if Caroline needed help.

Mark was annoyed. He had worked hard to keep his real identity from being found out. His mother, Sophie, had promised, but something had gone wrong with her in the past couple of months. She had begun acting strange, just like before the last fire. She had been lucky to get out alive and even more fortunate that no one had seen her going down the fire escape at the back of the house. She had staggered into the woods and he had found her lying by a stream.

They had spent the next two years of their lives putting back together the pieces and she had been doing really well. They had even located his older sister, who had been using a different last name, and she had helped with the rehabilitation. Mark had gone to school and finished a real estate course, and when he had seen the ad in the paper for a real estate agent in cottage country, he had applied. Mr. Donaldson had been quite taken with him and offered him a partnership after four months. It was a huge tragedy and loss for Mark when the old man took ill suddenly and then died. Mark was humbled at having been left the business.

He had been visiting his mother and sister when he received a call from Sally that Caroline had called. Mark had filled his sister in and left immediately. They had actually decided to postpone their move until their mother, who had come down with the flu, got better. Mark had thought his mother had been sleeping, but as he left, he noticed her looking at him. Her eyes had been glazing mad!

Mark was worried now. His sister had called him and said their mother had taken off with the car. Then she informed him she had gone off a few times and every time she returned, she had acted quite strange. She also told him their mother was having nightmares and was calling out names. Mark had recognized those names—they were the girls his mother had kidnapped. His sister said their mother was especially obsessed with two names in particular: Malcolm and Caroline!

Upon hearing that, Mark had jumped in his car and headed to Caroline's cottage. On the way, he called the police station and requested that a cruiser be sent out to 55 Deerfoot Lane. They told him one had already been dispatched there. His foot pressed down on the gas pedal!

Nathan noticed the glass on the porch. Someone had broken the window and then opened it to get into the house. He looked around nervously. He could hear a commotion inside. He was no hero, but if Caroline was in trouble, he needed to get in there, especially with all those murdered girls that had been found lately, and his grandfather's murder. He stepped through the window, dropping lightly to the floor. He wiggled toward an opening across the room and found himself in the kitchen. Nathan noticed a door that was slightly ajar. He stood and darted to it. Pausing a moment at the top of the stairs, he drew in a deep breath and then headed down.

The surprise that met Nathan at the bottom of the stairs sent excruciating pain into his foot. He screamed and fell to the floor. He could faintly hear what he thought was a roar, and then running feet before he passed out.

Caroline heard his scream and smiled. Did she dare to go and see who had broken into her house? Her father's traps had come in handy after all. She stood from her hiding spot and left the room, walking slowly to the bottom of the steps where Nathan was laying. His face was riddled with pain. As she knelt beside his body, an eerie feeling curdled in her blood. Suddenly a light from above washed over her. She looked at the top of the stairs, stood, and began to back away—back to the room and safety. She crouched in a corner, wrapping her arms around her legs.

"Caroline! Where are you? Come out, dear, I won't hurt you. I don't want to hurt you, Caroline. You were the prettiest of them all, you know. Caroline?"

There was a pause in which Caroline could hear the clicking of footsteps coming closer to the room.

"Caroline, don't be so difficult. You were difficult then, too, I remember, but I liked that in you. I forgive you, Caroline. I know it wasn't really you who brought the police to my house. It was that cop, Malcolm. But I've finally looked after him. Caroline? Do you want to know how I *did* him? It was easy for me. He was like mush in my hands, such a needy man. Of course, he was a too large for me to get into the boat by myself, so I had to call on a friend—the same one that helped me with the girls…are you still listening, Caroline?"

The footsteps ceased. The doorknob began to wiggle. Caroline drew in her breath. There was nowhere to run from this mad woman! She was trapped in the room. She looked around to see if there was anything she could use as a weapon.

"I know you're in there, Caroline. I can hear you breathing. I told you I wouldn't hurt you. Caroline?"

The door was opening.

"Mother!" A familiar voice rang out and another set of footsteps were fast approaching the room.

"Oh, Mark, I'm so glad you've come; Caroline is being difficult."

"Enough, Mother! This has to stop; you've gone too far."

The sound of an approaching police siren gave Caroline even more hope. She heard a car squeal to a stop and two doors slam. Heavy footsteps thundered overhead as the officers raced into the house.

"Mark, you need to help me get out of here!"

"I can't do that this time, Mother. You killed those girls and from what I heard as I came down the stairs, you also killed Mr. Malcolm. He was a cop, Mother—you murdered a cop!"

"Mark, please…"

"No, Mother…"

Caroline heard a guttural scream coming from the woman. She stood and raced for the partially open door, just in time to see the woman lunge at Mark, catching him off guard. He fell to the floor beneath the ranting mad woman. Caroline jumped on her back, trying to loosen her hold on Mark. Footsteps were running down the stairs. A flashlight beamed into the basement.

Officer Sarah raced to Caroline and grabbed hold of her wrist before she struck Mark's mother again. "It's okay, we'll take it from here. Jason! Cuff this woman!" she ordered as she put her arm around Caroline. "Come on, let's get you upstairs. It's over."

Mark was picking himself up. His face was lined with pain as he looked at his mother.

Sarah turned to him: "I think you have some explaining to do, sir."

He nodded.

Nathan, who had crawled under the stairs, groaned, bringing to the attention of the group that he was still there, and was hurt. Sarah took out her phone and dialled 911. "I need an ambulance to 55 Deerfoot Lane."

Princess was overjoyed to see Caroline. "That cat showed us where you guys were," Sarah pointed out. "She was pacing in front of the basement door, meowing like crazy." She motioned for Caroline and Mark to sit at the kitchen table. Sarah looked around at the mess before joining them. "I need to get your statements," she began, taking out her notebook. "Do you know if she had an accomplice?"

"She mentioned to me that someone had helped her to get Mr. Malcolm's body into the boat and that they had also helped her with the girls," Caroline began. "But she didn't say who it was—just that it was a friend."

Sarah kept asking questions and writing on her notepad. Soon, the ambulance arrived and Nathan was brought up the stairs and taken to the hospital. The paramedics had managed to get the trap off his ankle, but it would be a while before he would be able to walk on it.

Caroline grabbed hold of his hand before he was taken out of the house. "I'm so sorry, Nathan."

Nathan smiled sheepishly. "It's okay, you didn't know. Come visit me in the hospital?"

"I sure will." Caroline let go of his hand and then headed back to the kitchen.

Jason was waiting in the living room with Sophie. As Caroline passed him, he caught her by the arm. "Sorry I was so tough on you earlier; Malcolm was my friend."

"Don't worry about it. I understand. If it were me, I would have probably done the same," Caroline returned. She just wanted everyone to leave so she could relax with her Princess.

Sarah was still talking to Mark. He was looking down at the floor. His shoulders slumped forward, and his hands were twisting in his lap. He kept nodding his head whenever Sarah spoke.

The female officer looked up as Caroline approached the table. "You going to be okay out here all alone?" she asked.

"I'll be fine."

"I can stay the night with you if you like? With that broken window…"

"It's okay, I'll be fine. I'll call Mr. Calvin first thing in the morning to come out and fix it. I'll nail a piece of wood over it for tonight."

"The Department will pay for your window," Sarah added. She turned to Mark. "Well, that will be all for now, but don't leave town." Sarah closed her notebook.

Mark stood and approached Caroline. "Are you sure you don't want me to stay with you? I can put the piece of wood over the window…"

Caroline cut him off. "I'll be fine, Mark. I just need some time alone right now." She noticed the disappointment in his eyes as he turned and followed the police out of the house.

Sophie was directed into the backseat of the cruiser. Caroline stood watching from her doorway. Sophie had gone quiet, but as the car door closed on her, she turned her eyes toward Caroline. If hatred could be pure, it was the look that radiated through the window of the cruiser.

Mark paused at his car door, turned and waved to Caroline, who had stepped out onto the porch. "I'll call you," he shouted up to her.

Caroline smiled and waved. She watched the police car leave and sighed deeply. Mark was busy fiddling with something on his car's dashboard. Princess meowed for her mistress to come back in the cottage. As Caroline turned, she glanced down at the top step where she had left Mr. Calvin's file. It was gone!

She looked around nervously. All was quiet. Even the shadows. Caroline hesitated at the door. She heard Mark's car engine start. Quickly, she turned back and ran down the steps to his vehicle, and knocked on the window.

Rolling his window down, Mark smiled. "Change your mind about me staying?" he asked.

Caroline nodded, but for some reason was unable to speak.

Mark shut the engine off and stepped out of the car. As he went to put his arm around Caroline's shoulders, he noticed her shrink away from his touch. He dropped his arm back to his side. "Let's get that window boarded up," he suggested as they walked up the steps together."

Caroline just nodded again. As the door opened, Princess took one look at Mark, hissed, and raced up the stairs.

Flowers for the Attic

Linda had begun working as Mrs. Janson's personal companion in 1995. Mrs. Janson had been frail then, to say the least, but Linda never dreamed the old woman would live ten more years and that she would have such a fabulous time caring for her.

There had only been one strict rule—Linda was never to enter the attic. In fact, even if she had wanted to, the door was locked, and if there were a key, she was not privy to its location.

Linda travelled the world with Mrs. Janson during the first five years. Mrs. Janson loved to visit the beautiful flower gardens in different countries. In fact, she would bring home seeds, and Linda was instructed to plant them in the gardens surrounding the old mansion.

Linda laid her car keys on the kitchen counter and gazed at the emptiness. It was hard to believe Mrs. Janson was gone, and she had no idea what to do now. She'd decide after she spoke with Mr. Kennings, Mrs. Janson's lawyer. He had approached her after the funeral and said she was expected at the reading of the will at ten o'clock tomorrow morning.

Linda spent the evening packing her meagre possessions. The next morning she loaded her car and headed off to Mr. Kennings' office.

She was surprised to be the only person there. "Are there no others?"

"No." Mr. Kennings pulled a file from his drawer and set it on the desk.

"Strange, Mrs. Janson had several pictures of young women on the wall in her den. I just assumed they were nieces or relatives of some sort."

What happened next was even more shocking: Linda was named the sole recipient of an estate greater than could ever be imagined. "Sign here, miss," Mr. Kennings directed.

Linda drove back to the house, returned the suitcases to her old room and then wandered around, revisiting all the places where she had spent time with Mrs. Janson—where they had listened to music together, and where she used to read to the elderly lady. She had been a peculiar old bird, though, very secretive about her past.

"We should live only for the present," she would say, "because that is a gift. The past is gone, and the future is uncertain." She would smile, sip on her cup of tea and sit back in her old rocker, surrounded by the fragrance of fresh flower bouquets handpicked from her gardens.

Linda stopped by the den and gazed at the pictures. An eerie sensation crept through her bones when she saw a framed picture of herself hanging on the wall. It had not been there yesterday. She wondered who had hung it. To Linda's knowledge, no one else had been in the house for weeks.

She continued on, her steps leading to the once forbidden attic. As Linda drew near, she noticed the door was cracked open. *Strange, who could have opened this door? It has always been closed and locked.*

Taking no heed of her apprehension, Linda pushed it, and the creaking warned her it probably had not been used for some time. As the door swung open, an angel wing formed in the dust. Linda stepped over it, not daring to walk on an angel's wing.

She proceeded cautiously up the stairs, watching for broken boards, splinters, or nails. She noticed holes in the wall where there once must have been a railing.

Finally, the last step. Did she dare? What treasure awaited her—or would she only uncover the ghosts of lives lived long ago? Linda jumped—she was not alone! She thought she noticed a figure on the far side of the room. *Silly fool*—just a reflection in a mirror. Strange, though, how dust covered everything was, yet not the glass. She shuddered. Had someone managed to clean the mirror, yet not disturb anything else?

Linda meandered her way around the room, running her fingers along the dusty furniture; touching the soft, velvet clothing hanging in an antique armoire; eyeing the corner filled with old wooden toys—toys that had been meticulously crafted by someone's loving fingers.

What was that—there—in the middle of the room? A flower garden? Linda knelt down beside the enormous wooden barrels and touched the leaves of the plants. They were real enough. She dug her fingers into the earth and enjoyed the delicious aroma that floated into her nostrils. Strange, the flowers seemed to have been freshly watered. The blooms appeared ripe to be born. Linda observed the intense colours peeking from the buds.

She heard the door at the bottom of the stairs creak shut. Linda looked back and noticed her footsteps on the dusty floor had vanished. She stared up at the mirror. Mrs. Janson smiled and reached out her arms.

"Welcome, Linda, we have been waiting for you. Our garden is complete once again. Unfortunately, our previous white rose came to a most tragic end."

The mirror's reflection shimmered into the room. It stopped over the barrels of flowers and hovered there. Mrs.

Janson began to sing a sweet melody and the blooms began to grow and dance, drawing Linda into their loveliness. The last thing she heard was the gentle voice of Mrs. Janson: “Well done, Mr. Kennings.”

“Likewise, Mrs. Janson,” he replied.

The Witness

I've been around for 15 years and have observed a lot of things pass by my window. But on the night of Saturday, July 26, I witnessed a crime—in a roundabout way. Thank goodness I was there too, for, without my keen eye and superior intellect, the police would have taken forever to crack the case.

My name is Toby. I am a stout redhead—well, Jack Nelson, whom I share a house with, would consider me an overweight, orange tabby. He retired in April from the police force, which kind of upset my daily routine, but he does pay the mortgage, the household bills, and buys all our food. In turn, I reward him with affection when he most needs it. I especially enjoy it when he scratches behind my ears.

Jack has a friend—Mitch—a young man who'd been his partner during his last year on the force. Mitch has become a regular visitor, especially since his wife left him. My Jack didn't have a wife—guess I was enough for him. Well, there is a picture sitting on the mantle of him and a lady, but she isn't around now. Must have been before my time. Anyway, I don't really mind sharing Jack with others, especially if it is during my nap times. Jack is trying hard to help Mitch keep it all together.

"That boy has a short fuse," he told me one night. "Next time he comes over I think I'll tell him to get some counselling. He can't get over Yvonne leaving. Do you know what he said the other night, Toby?" I blinked. "Said he wasn't going to let her have his kids…said she was an unfit mother! I've never thought so…oh well, what you want to watch tonight, old boy? How about *Law and Order*?" I curled up beside Jack and closed my eyes. I knew it wouldn't be long before he joined me.

We were both startled from our nap by a loud knocking on the door. Jack staggered off the couch. "Who the heck can that be?" he grumbled. I stood up and stretched. Jack opened the door and Mitch stumbled in. It was obvious he'd been drinking.

"She's got a court order against me," he shouted. "I can't see my own kids unless I'm supervised!" He plopped into the La-Z-Boy chair. "Can I crash here for the night?"

"Sure, I'll get you a blanket." Jack returned a few minutes later and threw the cover on a snoring Mitch. What an interruption to an otherwise peaceful evening! "Keep an eye on him, Toby old boy; I'm heading off to bed."

In my opinion, Jack should have just shut the door in Mitch's face. I jumped up on the back of the couch and peered out my window. The usual nighthawks were staggering home from the bars. The joy of living downtown. Nothing out of the ordinary happening, though, so I may as well get some shut-eye.

I awoke to the sound of a loud crash of thunder and glanced at the La-Z-Boy chair. The blanket was still on the chair but I could tell it wasn't Mitch under it. Just to make sure, I made the leap and landed on a pile of pillows that had been arranged under the blanket. To an untrained eye, it could have been a body. Well, good riddance, I say; Mitch is exploiting too much of Jack's time now anyway!

I decided to check out my dish in the kitchen. All this extra responsibility of keeping a watch on things had made me hungry. Good man, my Jack; he'd remembered to fill it. Now, off to a proper bed. I jumped up carefully on the end of Jack's bed, made a little dough, purred softly so as not to wake him, then curled up and went to sleep.

The next morning I followed Jack into the kitchen. I rubbed around his legs and then ran to my dish, pointing out that it was empty. "You're eating me out of house and home, old boy," Jack laughed as he filled my dish. He turned the radio on…

"The police have put out an all-points bulletin for Yvonne Carter's two missing children and her husband, Mitch. The children were not in their room this morning and she believes her husband may have had something to do with their disappearance…"

"Hey, Mitch!" Jack walked into the living room and pulled the blanket off his friend. "I just heard the news—someone kidnapped your kids! Yvonne thinks you did it!"

Mitch leapt out of the chair. "What do you mean she thinks I did it? I've been here all night!"

I flattened my ears and glared at Mitch. What better alibi than a retired cop!

Jack returned from the kitchen with a cup of steaming coffee for Mitch. "Here, this will help calm your nerves," he said.

Nothing's going to calm his lying nerves, I thought, glaring at Mitch and switching my tail.

"Thanks, buddy." Mitch took the coffee. His hands were shaking—probably from guilt! "Who would have done something like that?" he asked. "I ain't got no money—not on my cop's wages. And how dare Yvonne think I would kidnap my own kids!"

Jack put his hand on Mitch's shoulder. "We'll get to the bottom of this. I'll give the Station a call…"

"No! No! They have an all-points on me; you can't let them know where I am." He paused. "I have to figure out what to do here."

Turn your lying self in! I hissed at Mitch as he reached over to scratch behind my ears.

"What's up, Toby? I thought you liked that?" Mitch was surprised at my reaction.

Not from you! I headed to the kitchen, stopping just inside the doorway. I turned and sat down, not wanting to miss a thing! I listened as Mitch cursed the system and Yvonne, as he repeated over and over that he had been here all night; how could he have kidnapped his kids? With every lie Mitch told, the hair on the back of my neck bristled.

Jack came into the kitchen. I raced to my dish. "No more food for you, old boy." Jack reached down and rubbed my back. "I have to go out for a bit; can you be nice to Mitch? He's hurting pretty bad."

Hurting, my back paw! Only thing going to be hurting on him is his conscience once I get finished with him! I growled and switched my tail furiously.

"What's wrong with you, Toby? Come on now, be nice." Jack grabbed his jacket from the hook by the back door and headed out. "Won't be long."

Mitch walked into the kitchen. I glowered at him. He reached down to pat me. I hissed. "What's the matter with you? Oh well, just a dumb cat!" he mumbled as he headed back to the living room.

I watched as Mitch picked up his jacket and headed for the front door. If he was going out, he was probably heading to wherever he had stashed the kids. I knew he was the culprit! I made a beeline for the door and as it opened, I managed to slip out unnoticed. I'll admit to you at this point that I have been an indoor cat for 15 years and it was a pretty strange world on the other side of my window, but I had to press on—the children's lives were at stake. Mitch looked around nervously and then strode quickly, heading north. I followed, close enough not to lose him, far enough back that I could slip quickly out of sight should he turn around. He went into a variety store and came out with a bag of something—food for the children, I presumed.

Mitch continued on, entering a part of the city where abandoned industrial buildings lined the sidewalks. He looked around furtively before opening one of the doors. I was too far away to slip inside before the door closed. I looked around and then noticed some boxes by the wall at the side of the building. A window was just above them. The ledge seemed wide enough.

I leaped onto the boxes and then to the ledge. The window was thick with years of factory grease. I pawed at the pane and cleared a small patch to peek through, just in time to see Mitch leaving a room. Something moved in the corner. I squinted my eyes and saw two little girls huddled on an old mattress. The variety store bag sat beside them. I flattened my ears and switched my tail. How could a father do this to his own children?!

Mitch stepped out onto the sidewalk. I jumped down from my roost but missed my target. Mitch swung around at the sound of me crashing into a garbage can. But, Lady Luck was with me: another cat skittered out from the boxes, giving me a chance to hide. I watched Mitch shrug his shoulders and heard him curse at the cat as it raced past him. He turned and headed off in the direction of Jack's house.

I followed as closely as possible, almost wishing I knew the great outdoors better because I might have been able to take a shortcut and beat Mitch home. Of course, I would have to figure out how to get back into the house. But the real concern now was to figure out a way to get Jack to where Mitch was hiding his two little girls!

I decided to wait by the back door for Jack. Hopefully he wasn't already inside, and with any luck I could slip in unnoticed. I curled up in the shade of a stone flowerpot.

"Hey there, old boy, how did you get out here?" A familiar voice woke me up. Jack opened the door. I ran to my water dish; detective business is thirsty work. Jack went to check on Mitch. I followed.

Mitch was sitting on the couch watching the local news on the television. "Hey, buddy, how are you doing?" There was genuine concern in Jack's voice.

"Not good. I don't know what to do!"

I jumped onto the coffee table and sat down right in front of Mitch. I flattened my ears, switched my tail, and growled.

"What's the matter with your cat, Jack? He doesn't seem to like me today."

You bet your black boot I don't like you, I glared.

Jack smiled. "Well, at the moment, I think it's because you are sitting in his spot." He paused. "I just came from the Station. The captain pulled me into his office; he suspects that I know where you are."

"Did you tell him?"

"No."

Oh, Jack, my dear friend, don't lie for this scumbag; don't ruin your perfect record. I made a leap for the back of the couch. Must be getting old, for I miscalculated my target and landed on Mitch's shoulder. My back claws dug in. Mitch yelled and then cursed as he noticed the blood seeping through his shirt. He raised his hand to swat me, but Jack grabbed hold of his wrist.

"Don't hit the old fellow; he didn't mean to miss the back of the couch."

I smiled triumphantly. Mitch stood. "I need to go for a walk," he mumbled, heading for the door.

Jack sat down on the couch. There was a puzzled look on his face. I crept onto his lap and began to purr. Jack scratched behind my ears. It was then that I noticed Mitch hadn't closed the front door properly. I jumped down from the couch, used my paw to pry the door open, and slipped outside. Jack gave chase, as I was hoping he would.

"Toby! What are you doing?"

I raced to the sidewalk, sat down, and waited. I could think of no other way to lead him to the children. Jack reached for me and then cursed as I managed to slip from his grasp. I headed down the sidewalk, meowing loudly and looking back to make sure Jack was still following.

Finally, I turned onto the street with the abandoned buildings, proceeding straight to the one where the girls were. I looked around. The doors were all shut tight. When Jack caught up with me, he was puffing. I hadn't realized what bad shape he was in! I darted for the boxes and made my way up to the window ledge. I meowed plaintively and pawed at the window.

"What are you up to, Toby? Something in there you want me to see?"

I continued meowing and paced the ledge.

Jack started to climb. "This better be worth it, old boy, or I'll be cutting your food in half!" Jack positioned himself firmly and peered through the window. "Oh my God!" he exclaimed. He reached into his pocket and pulled out his cellphone. "Give me Captain Morin!" he barked into the phone.

You should have seen the shocked look on Mitch's face when he opened the door and stepped out to a police escort. I sat proudly on the hood of one of the cruisers. Mitch glowered at me as the officer cuffed him. Jack raced into the building and returned carrying the two little girls. Yvonne came running toward her daughters and clutched them in her arms. She covered their tear-streaked faces with kisses.

Yvonne looked up at Jack. "I can't thank you enough."

"Don't thank me—thank Toby. He's the one who led me here." Jack walked over and rubbed behind my ears. I arched up proudly.

The next morning, a package arrived at the door. "It's addressed to you, Toby," Jack said as he opened the box. I stood on the back of the couch and peered into the box. Inside were various cat treats and a thank-you card with a picture of Mitch's two little girls on it. There was also a framed certificate: "This is to certify that TOBY is a Class-A Detective," Jack read. He chuckled and gave me a neck rub.

I blinked, lay back down, and closed my eyes. Detective work was pretty tiring, especially for someone my age. Hopefully, I could get enough catnaps in before the next big case came along!

The Coffin

It had been a quiet funeral. Marilyn put the key in the door of her new home. She'd had to sell the one she'd shared with George; too many memories kept her awake at night. This new home was old and small, but it had plenty of room for her. Marilyn wandered through the rooms. The previous owners had left the house quite clean. She peeked inside the kitchen cupboards; there were lots of them, just what she liked for all her collections of miscellaneous dishes that she assumed would one day either be grabbed up by her children or be sold at a garage sale.

Everything appeared to be in order, but there was one more place to check: the upstairs' room. Marilyn knew there would be one item up there—an old piano. She'd given her piano to her daughter because there was no sense in having two. She opened the door to the room and breathed in the scent of the antique mahogany. The piano had been recently polished. Well, she had to get going; tomorrow was moving day and she still had a lot of last minute things to do.

Marilyn worked tirelessly for two weeks, unpacking and putting everything in its place. The walls echoed loneliness, though. After 55 years of marriage, she was alone. Of course, there were the children and the grandchildren, but they had their own busy lives.

Marilyn decided it was time to check out the piano again. She stroked her fingers along the wood and then gently raised the keyboard lid. The keys were yellow, chipped, and dented from age. She played a few high notes, and then some bass ones.

"Funny," she mumbled, "it's been recently tuned."

Marilyn decided to test all the keys. Starting with the highest note, her fingers scaled away at the pain of her recent loss—down…down… What! Suddenly the notes refused to play. She tried again, adding extra pressure, thinking the section was just stiff from lack of use. Nothing!

Marilyn lifted the piano top, climbed on the bench and peered into the heart of the instrument. In its centre, she noticed a square box, and on it, a picture. She reached in and lifted it out. The picture was a painting of a young couple gazing dreamily into each other's eyes. She looked at the bottom of the box and saw an envelope: "*For Joslin,*" was written on it in a bold hand. Marilyn noticed it was not sealed. She took out the letter and began to read…

> *My dearest Joslin: how my heart aches at your passing. What a cruelty fate bestowed upon our love. I swore I would always keep you close to my heart and I would not have you entombed in the cold ground. I had you cremated and have placed your ashes in a spot that is almost as close to my heart as you. As my fingers race across the keys I hear your soft breathing in my ear; I hear your voice trill with excitement as you attempt the new aria I am playing. I feel your soul so close with every note I play. At first, I placed you on top of our piano, but no sound came from the keys, so I moved you inside to the heart of our music. I have asked my brother, Henry, to mingle my ashes with yours when my time comes. Until then, my darling Joslin. Forever yours, in life and death—Jonathan C. Smiley.*

Marilyn returned the letter to its envelope. She placed the box back in its resting place. Just as she was about to close the piano top she noticed the two intertwined hearts. The one read: *Joslin A. Smiley, 1853 – 1878*; the other read: *Jonathan C. Smiley, 1850 – 1885*. Beneath the hearts was an inscription: *May anyone who touches the keys of this piano, (lovingly crafted in this room by Jonathan C. Smiley, in the year of our Lord, 1873), be stirred by the music from its hearts!*

Marilyn sat down at the keyboard and let her fingers float over the keys. It was almost as though they had a mind of their own now—as if some beautiful magic had released their melody. And intermingled amongst the notes she heard a soft soprano voice singing an aria. Marilyn felt a tingling in her veins—everything was going to be okay. She played long into the night, her pain floating away with the notes. She knew that one day *she* would be reunited with the music of *her* heart—George.

Angelique

Ivan raced from the town. He wanted nothing to do with the preparations for the Valentine's Day celebrations. It had been two years since Gentile had died of some hideous disease, fading away as does a rose under the cruel frosts of fall. As he ran, he remembered the moment in the stable…

It had been the day after the Valentine's Day festivities; he'd met Gentile in the stable behind his grandfather's cottage. Her cheeks had blushed pink the moment she saw him and she had moulded into his arms.

"Oh, Ivan my love; my prayers were answered yesterday when you drew my name from the box. I laid the bay leaves on my pillow last night, one on each corner and one in the middle for my head to rest upon, and I prayed you would dream of marrying only me."

"That I did; the entire night," Ivan had breathed into her hair.

"And then, as you drew a name from the box, a flock of doves flew from the oak tree in the square. My heart beat with happiness, for my grandmother told me that when one sees the doves, it is a sign that they will be happily married. As I watched your face and saw it light up, I knew all would be well."

And all had been well—until Gentile had fallen ill a few months later...

Ivan, finally out of breath, stopped at the edge of the woods about a mile outside of his village. As he leaned up against a tree, he heard the music—haunting gypsy notes luring him into the woods. He hid at the edge of the clearing and watched her—mesmerized by the dancer that danced alone. The villagers feared the Gypsies, calling them tramps and thieves, but *she* looked like neither to him.

When she finished her dance, Ivan watched as she was escorted to a wagon just outside the circle. He stayed long enough to notice a burly man stand guard at its door. His heart moved like it had not done since professing his love to Gentile. He knew the Gypsies would be headed to his village and there would be a night of dancing and festivity. He would wait until then to profess his love to the Gypsy girl.

The Gypsy wagons rolled through the village on the eve of Valentine's Day. The villagers jeered them.

"Tramps!"

"Thieves!"

"Stay away you filthy Gypsies!"

"You'll have none of our children this time!"

Ivan sulked in a doorway, watching for *her* wagon, not wanting to take part in the radical crowd. He knew every one of the townspeople would attend the festivities later, no matter how they felt about the Gypsies. *Her* wagon was last in line—Ivan breathed a sigh of relief.

The wagons circled just outside of the village; hers, once again, sitting on the outskirts. Ivan made his way to the nearby grove of trees and waited in the shadows. It was some time before she appeared, but when she did, she walked straight toward him.

"Hello, boy," her voice was as musical as a waterfall on a balmy summer day.

Ivan blushed, unable to answer.

"What is your name?"

"I…I…Ivan," he gurgled.

"I am Angelique."

"That you are," Ivan whispered.

"Have you come to see me dance? You are early; I do not start until after dark."

Ivan blushed again.

Angelique placed a hand on his shoulder. Warmth surged through his veins. "Come, I will show you something."

She led him to her wagon. His knees shook as he climbed the steps. He glanced around furtively. She laughed. "My father is not here. He is preparing for tonight's festivities, which will be even more special tonight, being the eve of St. Valentine's. I am resting," she smiled seductively and closed the door.

Ivan's breath caught in his throat when he saw her portrait on the end wall of the wagon; she was in her dance costume. But, as stunning as the picture was, it did not do full justice to the beauty who stood before him.

Angelique's porcelain skin was touched with rose blossom accents high on her cheekbones, pointing in the direction of her mysterious chocolate eyes. Raven hair, braided with jingling beads, cascaded down her back, sweeping to the middle of her calves. The dress she wore stayed in place with a multitude of coloured ribbons wrapping around from beneath her bust line to the crest of her hips. The zenith of her breasts peeked precociously from the billowing material that covered most of her womanliness. Slender, well-muscled arms extended graciously from perfectly rounded shoulders and were adorned with numerous gold and silver bracelets. The bracelets were embedded with precious gems.

"You wonder why so many bracelets?" She smiled. "Each is a gift from every suitor who has ever thought themselves worthy of me." Her laughter tinkled in unison with the bracelets.

Ivan gulped.

"So, boy, why are you here?" the question was asked softly, yet with an authoritative air.

Ivan blushed.

"Speak, boy; I will not bite you."

"You are just so beautiful…"

"And what is beauty to you?" she interrupted.

Ivan was shocked at her question.

"This outer shell I have been cursed with?" Angelique turned away.

"I…I…"

"Are you no better than all the rest?" She turned back to Ivan, took hold of his hand, and placed it on her bosom. "Beauty is here, Ivan!"

Ivan felt the rhythmic beating of her heart beneath his trembling fingers. He knew that not just his face was beet red; he could feel the tepid flush spreading all through his body as his manhood intensified in its expectancy.

Angelique removed his hand and he felt the chill of loss. "Look around you; I am rich beyond measure with gold and silver and treasures, yet I have no one to warm me when I am cold, to hold me when I am sick, to comfort me when I am sad, to talk to me when I am lonely…"

"But all your bangles—surely, there was at least one amongst all those who was worthy!" Ivan managed to say.

"One." Angelique's eyes grew sad and her breath shuddered as she added, "but he did not give me a bracelet; he is the one who painted my picture."

"Where is he then?"

"We were to be married on Valentine's Day five years gone; he was found murdered that morning!" Angelique's eyes were glossy with tears.

Ivan felt her pain, remembering his own lost love. He reached out and touched her arm. "I am so sorry," he murmured.

Angelique looked deep into Ivan's saffron eyes. "I see you too have suffered." She stiffened. Voices were drawing close to the wagon. "Quick, you must go; my father returns." She moved a mat from the floor and pulled up a trap door. "I shall see you tonight?"

"Only death would keep me from you."

"I dance last, as always," she informed, as though the other entertainment should mean nothing to Ivan. The last thing he saw was her lips forming into a kiss, which blew his way. He reached up and caught it just as the trap door slammed shut.

From under the wagon, he heard the heavy footsteps of Angelique's father. "You have not slept, daughter," Ivan heard him say.

"I was restless, Papa."

"Still thinking of him?"

"Of course not, Papa."

"Good, he was not worthy of you; you know that, don't you?"

"Yes, Papa."

Ivan darted into the trees and then made his way home. He would return for her tonight, to see her dance and profess his everlasting love.

The villagers, despite their concerns, went en masse to see the entertainment, as Ivan had predicted. Of course, they bolted their doors and left some of the elders behind to watch for any unwelcome intrusions during the festivities. Ivan's grandfather was one of those men.

"Are you not going, boy?" he questioned his grandson. "You will miss the dancing girls. Maybe they can take your mind off Gentile. It has been long enough now, you need to move on!" the old man sighed heavily.

"I am leaving soon, grandfather."

Ivan took his time. There was only one dancer he had any interest in seeing. When he arrived at the Gypsy wagons, Ivan stood in the shadows, watching the merriment, his eyes searching desperately for Angelique. No sign of her yet. He sat down and leaned his back against a great oak tree and was just drifting off to sleep when the music stopped. And then…

"Ladies and gentlemen, now for the one you have all been waiting for—the one and only, Angelique!"

Sultry music was coming from the Gypsy instruments now—different from what it had been for the other dancers. Ivan stood up and stared, mesmerized by the vision before him. Angelique literally floated to the centre of the circle. Her feet did not appear to be even touching the ground, yet little puffs of dust created a steamy ambiance all around her.

Her arms moved with rhythmic fluidity, hypnotizing the watching crowd. Ivan walked toward her, drawn from his hiding spot to her beckoning arms. A flock of white doves flew from the trees; he smiled. Ivan stood before her as she danced—for him—for no one else—no one else mattered. Her body moved, swaying seductively within the centre of his arms, yet not a particle of their skin touched. The only sounds he could hear were the clinking of her bracelets and the lovely, melodious words she whispered just inches from his ears.

In the morning, the Gypsy wagons were gone. Ivan's grandfather was worried—his grandson had not returned home.

"I cannot remember even seeing Ivan there," one of the men mentioned.

"Those Gypsies—we should have known better than to trust them," someone else shouted.

"Our poor Ivan—such a gentle soul," added one of the women.

"It was a good night, daughter."

"Yes, it was, Papa."

"No regrets?"

"No, Papa."

Angelique gazed down at her wrist, at the newest bracelet—the one of silver embedded with bright purple and white stones with orange centres. Tears crept from the corners of her eyes. She was sad at how things had to be—but, she smiled as she stroked the bracelet and then raised it to her lips. At least, she and Ivan would be—*together, forever; my Valentine, my love.*

Master Arpeggio

Eliza smiled weakly. "I have something to tell you, Cindy."

"Later, auntie, you need to rest."

"You have a gift and he will teach you," she stated.

"What gift, and who will teach me?"

"Your voice, Cindy," Eliza sighed. "He is the Master."

"You have the beautiful voice, auntie—God given, my mama used to say."

Eliza pointed to her night table. "There is a brown envelope in there…"

"Auntie, you really must rest," Cindy insisted.

"I will rest later; now I must settle this matter. Pass me the envelope—it holds my will."

Cindy did her aunt's bidding.

"Now, pull up the rocker and listen carefully. I'm leaving you my home."

"But, auntie, surely there are others more worthy!" Cindy protested.

"The decision is not mine alone—this is a unique house."

Cindy thought her aunt was hallucinating. "The most unique entity in this house, Aunt Eliza, is your beautiful voice!"

"Remember the third floor, where you children were never allowed to explore?"

Cindy nodded.

"Now, I will tell you its secret…

"It happened when I came to Brantford. Your mother took me in. I'd had a breakdown while studying voice at the Toronto

Conservatory of Music and I had vowed never to sing another note as long as I lived!

"While walking one day, in an older part of town, I was drawn to a large brick house. A *for sale* sign was on the front lawn. I gazed up at the third floor and noticed a cat in the window. I thought this strange since the house appeared empty—who would leave their pet behind?" Eliza paused. "Hand me my juice, dear."

"I just knew I had to have that house," she continued. I used the money from my parent's estate to buy it. The first thing I did was venture to the third floor. I was surprised when I saw a grand piano, sitting in the middle of the room, with not a spec of dust on it. Also, on the wall, directly in front of the piano, were several portraits—all young women—watching over the instrument.

"I thought to call the realtor, but then, 'don't do that—the piano is for your lessons.' I was frightened! I called out, 'who's there?' and then this beautiful white cat appeared from nowhere and jumped onto the piano bench.

"Of course, not really expecting an answer, I asked the cat where his master was. 'I have none,' he answered. 'I am here to teach you. She,' his paw pointed to one of the portraits, 'has chosen you.'"

Eliza took another sip of juice, her hand shaking slightly as she returned the glass to her night table.

"The cat nodded his head. The piano opened. 'Let's hear your scales, Eliza,' he said. He waved his paw over the keys and the familiar scales I had been practicing for the past five years soared through the room. I opened my mouth and the notes came out, bright and clear, like never before. I glanced at the portrait and noticed the lady smiling at me.

"Finally, the piano stopped playing and the cat turned to me, 'not bad,' he said, 'we have a lot of work to do on the lower scales, though. Belinda had the same problem,' he pointed to the portrait. 'Be here tomorrow at 9:00 a.m. sharp—we'll practice till noon, take a break and then continue 'til supper.' As I turned to leave he said, 'by the way, you may call me Master Arpeggio.'"

Eliza leaned back on her pillow. Her face was ghostly. Cindy reached over and caressed her cheek. "Enough for today, auntie; you can finish the story tomorrow."

"There is no tomorrow for me, dear." Eliza reached for Cindy's hand, grasping it with her blue, spider-webbed fingers.

"Master Arpeggio told me it was time to choose my successor—I've chosen you. After the funeral, go up to the third floor, the key is in my safe. Go to him, my dear, and fulfill your dream."

"But, auntie, I'll never sing as well as you!"

"You will. Arpeggio will see to that. But, guard this secret with your life. When your time comes, you will have to choose your successor." Eliza closed her eyes.

Cindy sat with her aunt 'til the wee hours of the morning. She watched as her breathing became shallower. She stroked her cheek and whispered words of endearment. She sang their favourite song, *Evergreen*, and brushed away her dear aunt's final tears.

Eliza's funeral had been sparsely attended. Cindy's heart was heavy as she returned to the old house. She stood outside and stared up at the third-floor window. He was there—Arpeggio—she could sense him.

She made her way to the third floor. Upon entry, she saw a new portrait on the wall—a young Eliza. There was a charming smile on her lips.

"Well, shall we get started?" A handsome white cat was sitting on the piano bench. The keys began to play.

"As you wish, Master Arpeggio," Cindy said, then opened her mouth and sang like never before.

Five years had passed since Aunt Eliza's funeral. Cindy had excelled under the arduous tutelage of Master Arpeggio, amazing the greatest voices in the opera circles.

"Where did you come from?"

"What is your musical lineage?"

"Ah, you are Eliza's niece—that explains the familiarity!"

"Who did you say your teacher was?"

Cindy would smile and avoid that question, keeping well the secret of Master Arpeggio. But lately, a rumbling restlessness to know how Master Arpeggio had come to be kept pulling at Cindy, demanding an answer to this mysterious puzzle. Besides, how could she tell anyone who her tutor was—who would believe her instructor was a cat!

"Cindy—you are not focusing," Master Arpeggio spoke sharply.

"I am sorry, my mind wanders; I must ask you something."

Arpeggio knew the time had arrived for him to tell his story again. He jumped off the piano bench. "Follow me," he ordered.

Cindy followed him to a room off the studio. She looked around: three of the walls were hidden by books, stacked from floor to ceiling—many appeared to be time-worn. "This is my library," Arpeggio began, jumping onto a chair. "When I am not teaching, I like to read. Have a seat—what's on your mind?"

"How did you come to be?" Cindy questioned.

Arpeggio sighed deeply…

"It all began in 1694 when I was in service to a prominent Italian family. I was a Gypsy boy and had been left behind by my parents. They were singers with enchanting voices, so I was told, and they had no time to wait for me to recover from my illness, especially with audiences to please elsewhere.

"The family attended operas regularly. Their youngest child, Paola, was crippled from birth and had never known anything other than a wheelchair, or a sturdy set of arms to carry her. I was kept on after I recovered, for it was noticed how strong I was. One of my jobs was to carry Paola into and out of the opera houses. I was allowed to wait behind the curtain of the family's private box, and I would listen intently to the singers.

"My mind absorbed each aria like a sponge! When my household duties were fulfilled, I would head to the woods at the edge of my master's property and practice singing. I noticed my voice was easily trained and pleasurable to the ear—a bequest from my parents, I assumed.

"I began humming as I worked around the house. Paola loved to hear me and one day she requested I sing for her. I waited until no one was around. She was enthralled and demanded I teach her. I assured her I was no teacher, but she insisted—thus my first pupil."

"But how did you become a cat, and how have you lived so long?" Cindy asked.

"Patience, Cindy. Paola excelled with her singing! One day, we decided it was time she sing for her family. They were not as delighted as we expected—they loved opera, but not for their darling daughter! I was cast from the house. Paola's pleadings fell on deaf ears. We were devastated, Paola and I, for we were also deeply in love.

"I wandered aimlessly for weeks. One day I came upon a Gypsy fortune teller's shop. I entered and met Madame Fiona. She warned me that she was not just any Gypsy; she had great powers and I should be careful what I asked for. I had no money, but she didn't care—'sing Arpeggio,' she'd demanded. I was startled she knew my name.

"As I finished, she smiled and told me I was the one she'd been waiting for, and how it was foretold in Gypsy legends that there would come a young man with a voice so pure it would be as though the angels had touched his vocal chords. He would be a great teacher for centuries to come, but his life would be shrouded in secrecy.

"Madame Fiona told me how I could be with the one I loved, but it would be at a high cost. I told her I would do anything to be with Paola…"

Arpeggio had a faraway look in his eyes. He pointed to a single portrait mounted on the ceiling—a young woman in a wheelchair with a white cat sitting on her lap. "Paola," Arpeggio whispered. Cindy noticed tears trickling into the fur on his cheeks. "Upon her deathbed, she made me promise to continue teaching. As her successor, she chose a young woman she'd met in France."

"How did you come to Brantford?"

"I came here from Spain in 1902. Your aunt was chosen by Belinda DeSousa—how this happens, and all the other stories in between, are detailed in the diary. You may take it and read at your leisure." Arpeggio jumped down from his chair. "I am tired now; I'll see you in the morning."

Cindy found the diary on the shelf, and as she plucked the book from its resting place, she noticed Master Arpeggio disappear through the still-closed door.

Boarded Up

The final wooden sheet was nailed to the window of the old farmhouse. Kevin stood back and observed his handiwork. Three years were enough to have endured the trials he had suffered inside those walls. Of course, he wouldn't tell the realtor the reasons why he was moving; he would just say it was because of his health.

The wind picked up and was toying with the swaying branches of the willow trees that surrounded the property. The long-standing trunks creaked. The barn behind the house, empty now, moaned. A single, black crow cawed a good riddance to Kevin as he got into his car. He wondered if it was the same one that had greeted him on his arrival. Time would heal, with the help of Doctor Mona at the hospital. As he drove past the front of the property, he glanced at the For Sale sign and breathed a sigh of relief; maybe the next owner would have better luck.

Kevin was a walking bundle of nerves. Doctor Mona had suggested he check himself into the hospital for a few weeks, or for whatever it took to rid himself of his nightmares. She had also suggested he sell the property because it appeared to be the greatest source of his anxiety. He had finally decided to follow her advice—actually, he no longer had a choice.

His room was cold and impersonal. The walls were grey; the furniture was grey; the sky, outside the small window, was grey. Kevin's mood was black. He had been at the hospital now for three days and Doctor Mona still had not seen him. A nurse handed him a small white cup of pills three times a day, and he was expected to mingle in rooms filled with crazy people. He still hadn't written himself off as crazy yet, though.

Kevin heard footsteps approaching his door. "Good morning, Kevin," Dr. Mona entered his room. "Sorry I have not been in to see you yet. I trust they are treating you well here?"

Kevin wasn't sure what the proper answer was to the question—an answer that would not get him another dose of pills. "Yes," was what he decided.

"Good. Stella will bring you down to my office for ten o'clock so we can get started on your treatment."

"Doctor…" Kevin began.

"Save your questions for our session, Kevin. See you at ten."

Kevin paced back and forth across his room. "These damn pills are making me more edgy than I was when I was living in that house!" he muttered under his breath. At 9:55, Stella knocked on his door and entered without waiting for an invitation.

"Are you ready, Kevin?" Stella never smiled—not once in the three days he had been here—that he had noticed.

"Sure." Kevin followed her out.

Doctor Mona's office was large and had a huge window that looked out over the facility gardens. She was staring outside when Kevin entered. Stella directed him to a chair in front of the desk and then left. Finally, Doctor Mona turned around. Her face looked different somehow, Kevin thought to himself. There was a harshness to it that he had not noticed before. She smiled—maybe a hint of softness in her eyes. She sat down at her desk and took out a pen and paper.

"Let's go back to the beginning. Our phone session, before you came here, was quite informal, so I just want to check the accuracy of my notes." She paused. "When did you purchase the farm?"

"February 2006."

"Where was it you lived before?"

"Calgary."

"Why did you move to Brantford?"

"I was actually born here, so it is home to me. I met a girl in Calgary; she was from here too, and wanted to move back."

"Did she?"

"Yes."

"Before or after you did?"

"Same time."

"Did you live together?"

"For a time." Kevin sighed and stared out the window. The memory of Cara's exit was still painful.

"Whose idea was it to buy the farm?"

"Hers."

"But she left?"

"Yes."

An uncomfortable silence hung in the room. Doctor Mona tapped her pen on the pad of paper. She looked into Kevin's eyes—hers were grey and cold, like the furniture in his room. "Why did she leave?"

"She didn't like the house anymore—didn't like me anymore either."

"Why? What had changed?"

"You'll have to ask her."

Doctor Mona raised her eyebrows. "But you stayed."

"I had invested every penny I had on that property. It wasn't as easy for me to walk away."

"But you are walking away now."

"I no longer have a choice."

"Why is that?"

"The place is haunted."

Doctor Mona drew in a breath at the word haunted. "How do you mean *haunted*?" she queried.

"Is there another word I should use, doctor?" Kevin's words were tinged with sarcasm. "How about possessed, or ghostly, or eerie, or maybe preoccupied—yeah, that's what it is, or should I say, was—the house was preoccupied and whoever it was that preoccupied it decided not to leave!"

"Have you actually seen a presence in the house?" Doctor Mona questioned, ignoring Kevin's cynicism.

"Yes." Kevin winced, just thinking about the last sighting.

"Shall we talk about it? Where did you sense this presence?" Doctor Mona tapped her pen on the pad of paper. Her constant pen tapping was beginning to annoy Kevin.

"Everywhere." Kevin didn't think he was really ready to talk about the thing that was in the house. Not yet, anyway. The last episode had been too unsettling.

Doctor Mona noticed the tension in Kevin's face. "Maybe we should talk about that later," she suggested. "Tell me about your dreams. Where do they take place? Is the location always the same?"

"Yes…in the house…sometimes the barn…sometimes the woods beyond the barn…sometimes all three…but, yes, all there…on the property where that house is." Kevin looked down. He was shaking visibly now. He wanted some Scotch on ice, what he knew he would probably get was another pill!

"Are there people in your dreams?"

"Yes."

"How many?"

"Different each dream."

"Are any of them in all of your dreams?"

"Two of them—maybe. They seem to be the same, but I cannot ever see their faces."

"How do you know they are the same people then?"

Kevin shook his head. "I can't explain how I know, but I just know." Kevin hesitated and began rubbing his hands on the arms of the chair. "I think I would like to go back to my room now," he said. "I am tired."

Doctor Mona smiled and set her pen down. She picked up her phone and dialled. "Stella, could you please come and get Kevin…yes, give him an extra dose…no, that won't be necessary…no, I don't think he will be up for that…" Doctor Mona laughed lightly and then hung up the phone.

Once back in his room, Kevin curled up on his bed. He didn't want to close his eyes. He didn't want to face what it was his dreams would show him. But he did need to sleep. Maybe, the extra handful of pills Stella had given him would help.

Doctor Mona opened the door to her red Corvette. Just as she was ready to slip inside, Stella came running up to her.

"Doctor, a word with you please."

"What is it, Stella?" Doctor Mona really did not like Stella; the woman was irritating. She was nosey too—too nosey. She would have to start thinking about replacing her soon. But that wouldn't be an easy thing to do, especially now that the workers had unionized a few months ago.

"I gave Kevin the extra pills you ordered, but I think maybe it was too much medication for him? He doesn't really seem all that disturbed, not like some of the others here."

Doctor Mona's muscles tightened. How dare this nurse question her orders! "On the contrary, Stella," a rigid smile accompanied the words, "he was quite disturbed when he left my office." She paused. "Is he sleeping now?"

"Yes, still."

"Good. If he sleeps through supper, make sure you leave orders for him to get something to eat later. I don't want him woken up. Will that be all, Stella?" Doctor Mona's words had a dismissal tone to them.

"Yes, doctor." Stella turned and headed back to the hospital.

Doctor Mona got in her car and drove off. She was upset at the delay. She was supposed to have met Joe at 5:00. Joe did not like to be kept waiting. She hoped he would still be there. She pressed her foot harder on the gas pedal. Her knuckles turned white on the steering wheel. The car finally reached the dirt road. She turned onto it and slowed down. There were too many potholes. As she approached the farmhouse, she noticed Joe's car was still in the driveway.

Just as she pulled her Corvette to a stop beside his car, Joe walked around the corner of the house. "About time you got here," he yelled to her. "I was just about ready to leave."

"I was delayed at the hospital. Stella thought I was giving Kevin too many pills."

"You are going to have to do something about her, Mona."

"I know."

"Well, let me show you the house."

Kevin woke up from his drug-induced sleep. He didn't feel any better, in fact, he felt worse. His head was pounding; his body felt like a piece of lead. Even through his haziness, he was beginning to regret having come to this hospital. He should have just closed up the house and walked away from it. Kevin was starting to think that if he had just done that, he would have been okay.

He glanced at the side-table by his bed and noticed a sandwich and a glass of orange juice had been left there for him. Ignoring the food, Kevin got out of bed and walked over to the door. He turned the doorknob. It was locked. Of course, he thought as he looked at his window, it was dark outside. Everything in this place shut down before the sun set. He sat down on the edge of his bed and picked up the plate. Kevin unwrapped the sandwich and began to nibble at the crust. It was dry. He took a sip of juice. It was warm. He wasn't really hungry anyway.

Kevin walked back over to the door and jiggled the knob. He knocked, hoping someone would be walking by. Then he remembered that he had a buzzer that was to be used should he need something, and he needed to get out of the room for a few minutes. He pushed the button. He waited. And waited. Finally, he heard the lock click and the door opened. An unfamiliar face stepped through the doorway.

"What can I do for you, Kevin? Is something wrong?" The voice was pleasant enough.

"I would just like to take a walk down the hallway. I have been sleeping for a while and need to get out of this room," Kevin said, hope clinging to his words.

"I'm afraid I cannot do that, Kevin. You know the rules; no one leaves their rooms after 9:00. I did bring you your pills, though. Stella left orders that if you woke up, I was to give them to you."

Kevin was angry. "I don't want any more pills. I've had enough of your pills. They don't make me feel any better. All I want is to take a walk down the hallway!"

"I can't let you do that. Now please, here are your pills…"

Kevin's hand smacked the pills from the nurse's hand. They scattered on the floor. He was proud of himself for that move—until her hand reached to a device she had clipped to her belt…

"Cameron, I need your help in room 86; Kevin is becoming violent!"

Kevin started to laugh. He was backing away from the nurse as Cameron came bursting through the door. Kevin swallowed hard. What had he done? Cameron was holding a needle in his hand.

"What's the matter, Sophie?" he asked.

Sophie pointed to the pills on the floor and then to Kevin, who was still laughing.

"I see," Cameron said. "Settle down, Kevin. If you don't take your medication one way, we have other means to give it to you." He waved the needle in the air as he advanced toward Kevin.

Kevin threw his arms up in the air. "Okay, okay, I'll take the pills."

"Too late. They are all over the floor now. This needle will do the job." Cameron had reached Kevin by this time and taken hold of his arm. The needle was sinking into his flesh before Kevin had time to protest further. He felt himself being directed back to his bed…felt his body flop down on the lumpy mattress…felt himself fading away…saw the blackness coming…

Stella was troubled. She had never really liked Doctor Mona, couldn't put her finger on the exact reason. Things had changed since the doctor had come to the hospital five years ago. Darkness always seemed to be lurking around every corner. Many of the patients that had been admitted were not really all that bad off. In Stella's opinion, most of them shouldn't even have had to be admitted; they could have just done day-programs.

But Doctor Mona insisted on in-house treatments. Stella had noticed that many of them got worse as time went by, staying much longer than should have been necessary. And now there was Kevin. Stella felt he didn't really need all the medication that was being pumped into him. She would address the issue again tomorrow with Doctor Mona.

"Thank-you, Joe. The house is perfect, but I am not quite ready yet to put an offer on it." Doctor Mona smiled.

"Better not wait too long, Mona. Properties like this are in big demand. You know what happened with the last place you waited on?"

"That won't happen again, though, will it Joe?"

Kevin's nightmare returned in full force. The eerie, misty figure hovered over him. A high-pitched groaning sound pierced his ears. He felt cold, even though he was sweating. The figure was joined by another, and another, until there were five of them—all faceless. And then he was not in his bed anymore—he was running toward the barn, the apparitions close on his heels. Finally, he reached the barn door. He tried to open it. The handle was crusted with rust. He heard someone laughing. Suddenly, the door gave way and Kevin stumbled inside. He turned, trying to shut the spirits out, but they pushed through, still groaning. He fell backward. A hand reached out to him—a real hand.

"Let me help you."

Kevin looked up into Doctor Mona's eyes.

"There, that should settle you. I don't understand why you weren't resting with the amount of tranquilizer I prescribed," Doctor Mona said as she left the room.

Joe was tiring of Mona's game. He had thought that by now they would have realized a lot more money. He was beginning to wonder if she was actually doing the split according to their agreement. This was the tenth house they had turned over and he had yet to see $100,000 in his account. She was driving a new Corvette; he was driving a six-year-old Buick. She was living in the last house they had turned over—a real beauty. He was living in a one-bedroom apartment. She kept telling him a lot of the money was going into repairs; it wasn't her fault the houses needed so much work to bring them up to par for resale. He had trusted her enough, up to now, not to ask for receipts. Now, Joe was glad that he had secured himself a bit of collateral.

Doctor Mona placed the phone back in the receiver. Meagan was getting greedy. If she asked for anything more, Mona was going to have trouble explaining to Joe why he wasn't getting as much as he thought he should. He was not a stupid man, and he was the realtor who set up and closed all the deals. He knew the profits they were realizing.

Of course, Meagan said that it was she who took the biggest risk, setting the houses up for the new owners. And, her equipment was not cheap. Mona didn't understand why Meagan couldn't just reuse most of it. Meagan had also pointed out that she took an even bigger risk because sometimes she had to get back into the houses to move things along.

Meagan stopped her car at the back of the farmhouse. There were a few items she needed to retrieve. She laughed as she packed her special equipment, the same stuff she used over and over. Her bank account was well over $100,000 and it was almost time to pack up and get on with her plans.

As Meagan drove home, she smiled, remembering the look on Mona's face when she had stopped by for a glass of wine after seeing the house last night. "This tastes weird," Mona had said. Meagan had assured her partner it was fine—maybe just a bit off because she had opened the bottle the night before.

Doctor Mona threw her keys on the kitchen table. Her stomach had been bothering her all day. Actually, ever since she had drank the wine at Meagan's house last night. She was tired too, not having slept well—bothered by weird dreams. She threw a frozen dinner in the microwave and picked up the phone to call Joe. She wanted to know how it had gone with Stella. At first, Joe had been hesitant to do away with the nosey nurse, but Mona had insisted she was becoming a problem and now that they were close to clearing out and getting away with everything, she couldn't take a chance on Stella going to the police with her suspicions.

Joe answered on the fifth ring. He assured Mona that everything was looked after, but he also insisted that they get the deal done. He pushed her for an answer as to how many more houses before they could get to that tropical paradise she was always dangling in front of him.

As Doctor Mona crawled into bed, she was wondering just how long she could keep up this charade. Joe and Meagan were becoming problematic. She had done her best to make sure they had never met, but that was getting tricky. And those two individuals meeting was something Doctor Mona definitely did not want to have happen!

Stella found herself waking up with a horrific headache. She was lying on a cot in a small, windowless room in a basement. There was a dim light on a bedside table. She noticed a note. *Make yourself at home; you will be my guest for a while. There is food and drink in the small fridge in the corner of the room, enough to keep you going until I return. Don't bother trying to escape, I've locked the door from the outside. Don't worry, if you do as I say, you'll have nothing to fear.*

Dr. Mona was late for work again. She had been up three times in the night, each time with worse stomach pains than the time before. When she arrived at her office, she was pale and still shaking. She looked over her appointments and then picked up the phone and called the nurses' station.

"I need to cancel all my appointments for today," she said to the nurse who answered.

"Shall we reschedule them for you?"

"No, I shall do that myself. I am not feeling well, so think I am just going to go back home. I'll call you later to let you know if I will be in tomorrow." Doctor Mona hung up the phone.

As she was leaving, Doctor Mona thought to check in on Kevin, but as she neared his room a wave of nausea swept over her and she headed to the washroom instead. She splashed cold water on her face and looked in the mirror. The circles around her eyes were dark, her skin pale. When the queasiness finally subsided, she made her way out to her car, forgetting all about Kevin.

Doctor Mona backed her car out of its parking spot. As she drove past the visitor parking section, she noticed a familiar vehicle—a black SUV with a personalized licence plate—SHOCKER. What was Meagan doing at the hospital! Doctor

Mona hit the brake, put her car into reverse, and returned to her parking spot. She rushed back to the hospital and headed straight for Kevin's room.

Meagan had decided to step things up a notch. She had actually observed Kevin during one of the times she had been in the farm house. She had been caught off guard when he had come home early from work. He wasn't like most of the other ones. In fact, she had gone back several times, after the girl had left, and had just sat and observed Kevin from one of her hiding spots. He was nice—good looking too. And she had decided it was time to move on, and have someone in her life.

When Meagan had asked the nurses which room Kevin was in, and had told them she was his sister and that she had just found out he was in the hospital, they seemed relieved that someone was finally coming around to see him. They all thought he was a real nice guy. Meagan had asked if she could take him out for a walk and they had seen no reason why not. One had even mentioned that the fresh air might do him some good.

Meagan was pushing Kevin out the back door of the hospital as Doctor Mona ran in the front door. As Doctor Mona was entering Kevin's room, Meagan was helping Kevin get into her SUV. As Doctor Mona was racing back to her car, she caught sight of the black SUV leaving the parking lot. Meagan glanced in her rear-view mirror and saw a very frustrated Doctor Mona standing in the parking lot.

Kevin groaned. He didn't want to ask this young woman what was going on yet. He was aware of only one thing: she, for some unknown reason to him, was getting him out of the hospital, and that was what he wanted.

Once she was home, Doctor Mona picked up the phone and dialled Joe's number. When he answered: "We have another problem," she said. She explained to him that Kevin wasn't in the hospital anymore. Someone, posing as his sister had taken him out. "No," she had lied; "I have no idea who it was. I didn't know he had a sister."

"Well," Joe returned, "maybe we should just forget this house, pack up, and get out of here."

"This is the last deal, Joe. That house will turn over a profit like none of the others have. I need you to draw up the paperwork, with the figure we already discussed. When I find out who this sister is and where she has taken Kevin, I will get back to you."

After Doctor Mona had finished her conversation with Joe, she called Meagan's number. Meagan answered on the first ring, as though she were expecting the call. "What the heck are you doing, Meagan?" Mona screamed into the phone.

"Is there a problem?" Meagan's voice sounded strange. "Are you feeling okay, Mona?"

"I'm fine. I just want to know what you are doing with Kevin!"

Meagan's laughter rippled over the phone line. "Making a deal, my dear doctor—making a deal." The line went dead.

Meagan walked back into her kitchen, where she had left Kevin sitting at the table while she had taken Mona's call. She turned the coffee pot on and after Kevin had drunk two cups of coffee, his head began to clear. "Who are you?" he asked. "And why did you get me out of the hospital?"

"First of all," Meagan began; "I want to let you know that what has been happening to you was really not of my doing, initially..."

"Initially…happening to me…your doing…" Kevin interrupted.

"Let me explain. Doctor Mona has had a scam going for the past five years. She scopes out houses that she wants to *turn over*, as she puts it, and then she sends me in to wire the place up for the new owners."

"Wire…"

"Just let me finish, Kevin. I go in and wire the place with ghostly sounds and images. The haunting is initiated slowly, increasing intensity as time goes. Usually, the new owners leave quite quickly, but you stayed longer than most, so I had to intensify the happenings. After your girlfriend left, I used to hide in the house and watch you—she wasn't good enough for you, you know." Meagan reached out a hand and touched Kevin's arm. He flinched. She shrugged.

"Anyway, you finally left and Doctor Mona admitted you to the hospital, just like she admitted all the others—some are still there, you know. It is easy for her to manipulate her patients with drugs and keep the hallucinations alive. When she talks to them about the house they just left and finds out that it is haunted, she acts shocked and then she slowly convinces them to put it on the market and sell it. She has a real estate guy working for her; doesn't know that I know who it is, though. She thinks she has kept us secret from each other. He is taken with her. I have watched the way he looks at her. Poor sod! Doctor Mona gets him to set the price of the house far below its market value and then she swoops in and buys the property. Someone goes in to clean it up and do any necessary repairs, and then she resells it, turning over a substantial profit."

"Which she gives you and the real estate guy a portion of," Kevin stated.

"Yes."

"So what makes you think I won't turn you in right now? Why are you telling me all this, incriminating yourself in such a scheme?"

"I want to make a deal with you. I have been quite successful in putting away my portion, plus a little added bonus money for supplies I told Doctor Mona I had to buy. I have a substantial sum of money in a bank on an island where time is of no essence. I'd like you to join me there."

"You don't know me. Why would I want to do that? Why would I even be stupid enough to trust you?"

"First of all, I do know you. Remember, I have been watching you. Second, I am ready to settle down and I am tired of the single life—I kinda like you. Third, wouldn't it be nice to take revenge on Doctor Mona for what she has put you through?" Meagan leaned in closer to Kevin. He got a whiff of her perfume. It smelled good.

"But you were part of it!" Kevin stated matter-of-factly.

"True." Meagan was going to have to tread carefully with her words. "But, I am not the mastermind, and I have wanted to get out of this for quite some time—just didn't know how." She tried to look depressed about the entire ordeal.

Kevin was wondering when his nightmare was going to end. "I'll have to think on this. It is a lot for me to absorb." He paused. "So do you believe you are going to get away with all this once you expose her? Won't she turn you in as well?"

"We'll be long gone, Kevin, and she will have no clue where. Once we are out of the country, she is not going to pursue me, right? That would be incriminating herself."

"What about the real estate guy?"

"He is not of our concern. Anyway, I should let you sleep on this." Meagan stood up. "Follow me, Kevin; I will show you your room."

Joe opened the door to the room in the basement. Stella was sleeping on the cot. He walked over to her and gently shook her shoulder. She opened her eyes and moved away from him, cowering in the corner.

"Who are you? What do you want with me?" she yelled, her voice hoarse.

"My name is Joe, and I want to make a deal with you."

Stella listened as Joe told her about Doctor Mona's scheme. But even with his confession of his part in the plot, she was wary. She had secured her own bit of collateral, which of course was something she was not going to mention—yet.

"Why did you save my life?" Stella asked.

"Whatever my part in this has been, it was only done for the money," Joe answered. "When the good doctor asked me to get rid of you…well, I draw the line at murder. I had no choice but to take matters into my own hands and end this."

"But won't exposing her get you sent you to prison, as well?"

"I'll be long gone from here. I think Doctor Mona has been cheating me of my share of the profits, but I figure I have enough to start over somewhere else. There are a lot of places where I could disappear and use my real estate skills to make a living."

"I see." Stella had no idea where this conversation was going, nor did she have any intention of fully trusting this man. Even though he hadn't killed her as Doctor Mona had suggested, there was no actual concrete proof Doctor Mona had asked him to kill her—only his word. At the moment, she would just have to play along, gain his trust, and then try and escape.

"So, where do I fit into all of this?" she asked.

"I need a few days to get my stuff together and prepare my exit from the country. Before I leave, I will give you the key to a safe-deposit box at a bank here in town. Inside that box is everything you will need to have Doctor Mona convicted of the crimes she has been committing over the past five years. As for me, I will be long gone—no trace of me whatsoever."

"What makes you think I won't tell the authorities about you? They have their ways of tracking people down you know."

"I think you are a person who rewards one good deed with another. I saved your life; now I am asking you to turn and look the other way while I save mine. Doctor Mona is the actual mastermind behind this. I believe she has just used me to get the deals through, and, like I said before, she has a lot more cash than I do. For that matter, probably more than any other person she may have dragged into this. I am not stupid enough to think I am the only player in her game; I just don't know who else is in on it."

"I'll need some time to think about this." Stella pulled the blanket up to her chin. She was cold.

"Don't take too long, Stella; I'd like to be gone by the end of the week."

"And if I decide not to help you?"

"You'll help me. You are a nurse. You like to help people. In that safety-deposit box is a list of the names of all the victims, some of who are still in the hospital where you work."

"I see."

"I'll check in on you later," Joe said as he turned to leave. "Anything I can get you?"

"A key to the door." Stella forced a smile.

Doctor Mona picked up the phone, called the hospital to say she wouldn't be in again, and then called her doctor. She could not shake whatever had overcome her. Nothing she ate stayed down. Her head was spinning unmercifully, and not just from the illness. She was beginning to worry about the situation she was finding herself in. Meagan's apparent exodus was a problem Doctor Mona hadn't expected to have to contend with. What kind of a deal was she making with Kevin? And how could she do that without incriminating herself? Doctor Mona was also no longer sure of where Joe stood. He had become whiny of late, just wanting to pack up and go to that island she had dangled in front of him. The man was clueless. She had never had any intention of going anywhere with him!

Kevin paced back and forth in the room Meagan had shown him into. "What do I have to lose?" he muttered to himself. "Doctor Mona has destroyed my life for no reason other than greed. I wonder how many others she has destroyed. But, do I trust Meagan? I don't really know her. Maybe it's better to trust the devil I know more of than the one I know less of."

Kevin lay down on the bed and waited for the dreams to come. He slept.

The envelope marked "Confidential/Urgent" arrived by special courier. There was no return address. Brian Ritchie, the hospital administrator, opened the letter and began to read. With each sentence, his frown deepened. When he was finished, he sat for a moment, pondering his next step. Should he call Doctor Mona and confront her with these allegations, or should he inform the Board first? Doctor Mona had come highly recommended, and she had been with the hospital for six years. On the other hand, Stella had been with the hospital for 30 years. Brian knew her well and could not fathom her making up a story like this. He picked up the phone to call Stella and ask her why she hadn't come directly to him. Then, he would pay a visit to the hospital and drop in on Doctor Mona.

Doctor Mona's physician sent her for blood tests to investigate what her problem might be. He advised her to take a couple of days off work, eat light foods, and get plenty of rest. She left his office and headed to work. She couldn't afford to take any more time off, regardless of how ill she felt. Her patients needed her care, and she had some issues that needed to be dealt with—Joe and Meagan being two of them. And, Kevin, if she could get to him, being the third.

Kevin couldn't remember when he had slept so well. He walked over to the door and tried to open it. Why would Meagan lock him in? He walked over to the window and looked out. There was a black SUV in the driveway. He glanced around the neighbourhood—not a soul in sight. He jiggled the window to see if it would open. Finally, it gave way. He removed the screen and looked down. There was a flower bed under the window. He began to crawl through the opening. It wasn't that far to the ground.

Joe had already packed what few things he was taking with him. He double-checked his personal papers and then drove to the office to draw up the offer on Kevin's house. He didn't want Doctor Mona to suspect anything. From the office, he returned home, called the airport and booked his flight. Then Joe sat down at his desk and began writing. When he finished, he sealed the letter in an envelope, addressed it to Stella, and headed to the bank to put it in his safe-deposit box. He also closed all his bank accounts. Two more days and he would be long gone from this place. Joe took out his cellphone and dialled the hospital.

"Doctor Mona, please."

"I am sorry, the doctor is busy, sir. Would you like her voicemail?"

"Sure." Joe was actually relieved he wouldn't have to talk directly to Doctor Mona. He waited for the beep. "Hey there, Mona, the offer is drawn up and waiting for you at the office. I instructed Cindy on what you have to do. I have to show some properties down by the lake today. Talk to you when I get back."

Brian didn't get an answer at Stella's house. "Of course," he mumbled to himself, "she'd be at work. I'll touch base with her there before I speak to Doctor Mona."

When Brian talked to the nurses, he was surprised to learn that Stella hadn't shown up to work for three days. It was so unlike her, they told him. One of the nurses said that she was going to stop by Stella's house after her shift. Brian told her he would do that now. As he was leaving the wing, Doctor Mona stepped out of her office. She walked over to the nurses' station.

"What was Mr. Ritchie doing here?" she asked.

"Looking for Stella."

"Where is Stella, anyway?"

"We don't know; she hasn't been in for three days—hasn't even called."

Doctor Mona attempted a show of concern. "That is so unlike, Stella."

"Sure is. Mr. Ritchie is going to stop by her house and check on her. She's no spring chicken, maybe she had an accident."

"Well, if she has abandoned her job, we will have to find a replacement." As Doctor Mona turned and walked back to her office, she heard one of the nurses say, "cold one, that doctor is." As she shut her office door, Doctor Mona wondered what the Chairman of the Board wanted with Stella.

Brian peered into Stella's kitchen window. There were no lights on, but he noticed her purse on the floor and its contents were scattered all over. He took out his cellphone and called the police.

Meagan decided to check on Kevin. She hoped he was going to play along with her plan—not that she intended to stay with him forever, but it would be nice to have someone around for a while. She opened the bedroom door. The window was open; the room was empty. She raced downstairs and out to her SUV. "He can't have gotten too far yet," she muttered under her breath.

Even though it was a long trek, Kevin had managed to find his way to the police station. As he was racing up the steps, a police car squealed out of the parking lot. "Never a dull moment," he thought. At the front desk, Kevin explained that he had some valuable information. Within minutes, a detective took him into a side room.

Kevin quickly spilled everything he knew. He had the feeling that once Meagan discovered he was gone, it wouldn't take her long to disappear.

Doctor Mona's stomach began to churn again. "Enough of this," she moaned as she picked up her purse and headed out the door. On her way past the nurses' station: "Cancel the rest of my appointments for today," she barked.

The on-duty nurse looked up. "Are you okay, Doctor? You look so pale."

"I'll be fi…" Doctor Mona collapsed.

Joe was sitting in a coffee shop when a young woman entered. He was surprised when she headed straight for his table.

"We have a mutual acquaintance," she said as she sat down across from him. "Which means we have a mutual problem, Joe."

"How do you know who I am?"

"I make it my business to know things," Meagan returned.

"Who is our mutual friend?"

"Doctor Mona."

"So my gut feeling was right; there were others."

Meagan smiled and sat down. After half an hour they stood up and shook hands. "That won't be a problem," Joe said. "All my stuff is ready; I'll just change my flight and meet you at the airport in one hour."

The police cruiser stopped in front of Stella's house. Brian was waiting on the front step. One of the officers picked the lock and then they all rushed in. The kitchen was a mess. As Brian looked around, he noticed a business card on the side door landing. "I think we might have something here," he yelled to the officers.

Joe was running down the steps to his apartment. He would grab his stuff and then tell Stella he would call someone to come and get her once his plane was ready to take off. Just as he was headed to the room where he had locked Stella, Joe heard the police siren in his driveway. He dropped his suitcase on the floor, sat down and waited.

When Meagan called the hospital to talk to Doctor Mona, she was informed the doctor had just been rushed to the Medical Centre. She was asked if she was a family member or a friend. Meagan smiled. "I am the closest thing to family Doctor Mona has ever had," she answered and then hung up the phone.

Meagan had convinced Doctor Mona, not long after they had met, to name her as the beneficiary of her estate. Doctor Mona, who had no family, decided she had to leave her money to someone—why not someone who would have been the perfect daughter, had she had one. Meagan had arranged with her lawyer to act as a proxy for any legal matters that might come up, telling him that she would be traveling for a couple of years to some very remote places. He had her instructions; she would contact him. Meagan looked around her apartment. It was spotless. She picked up her suitcase and headed for the airport.

"Joe spilled his guts," the officer grinned at Meagan. "Told us you put the poison in Doctor Mona's wine that night." He leaned toward her. "Oh yeah, we had to upgrade your charges to murder—hospital called—the good doctor just died."

"Can't take Joe's word; he set up all the deals," Meagan's tone was sarcastic.

"Maybe not, but we can take Kevin's, and Stella's."

"Kevin…Stella?"

"Yeah, you know…Kevin and Stella. Stella came to us a couple of years ago, suspicious about some things going on at the hospital. Doctor Mona was a smooth operator, though. Kevin just happened by; he was young and naïve, the perfect patsy for Doctor Mona to hone in on! He agreed to help us out if we could drop a misdemeanour he had on his record. He played the part brilliantly." The officer smirked. "Not so cocky now, are you?"

Meagan slumped down in the chair and closed her eyes. What the heck—she'd still be young when she got out. If she pled temporary insanity, she'd be out in ten years—maybe less.

Meagan smiled. The money was securely locked away. She sat up in her chair, pulling her knees to her chest and rocked back and forth. She began to hum an old nursery rhyme. *May as well start from now—no witness like a cop to testify as to how insane I am...*

The Gardeners

Betty was celebrating her 65th birthday and her friends had bought her a landscaping certificate. “We’re tired of hearing you complain about your flower beds,” Mildred commented.

“So, we thought we’d do something about it,” Gwen added.

The three women had been friends since childhood, sharing both good and bad times. They’d all become teachers: Mildred had taught business; Gwen, math and science; and Betty, English. Mildred and Gwen always laughed when Betty mentioned she was going to write a great Canadian novel one day.

None of them had married. Well, Mildred almost did, but her beau was killed in a car accident just weeks before the wedding—she never fully recovered, mentally. Gwen used to say to Betty—on the side—that she thought Mildred was a bit touched in the head.

Betty took a sip of her tea and looked at the gift certificate. She didn’t recognize the company name. “Are these local people?” she asked.

“Just moved to town about a month ago,” Mildred replied.

“We got a deal,” Gwen added. “Looks like some young fellows just trying to get their business going.”

“They showed us some pictures of gardens they’ve done in other towns,” Mildred mentioned.

Gwen’s voice became serious. “I was a bit hesitant at first. The fellows sitting in the truck—two of them—looked a tad too shady, but the one at the door was clean cut, and very polite.”

"I was having tea with Gwen that day," Mildred intervened. "I didn't like the looks of the fellows in the truck either—I was peeking through the living room curtains—but, like Gwen said, the sales fellow was quite striking."

"Bottom line is, we got a deal; you can get your garden done, Betty, and we can have some peace from your nagging about not being able to do it yourself!" Gwen set her teacup on the coffee table. "Well, I gotta get going; Buster will be wanting out for his afternoon business." Buster was Gwen's cocker spaniel; she'd left him home today.

"I better move along, also," Mildred said. "Prince will be missing me." Prince was Mildred's poodle; she'd left him home, as well. Gwen and Betty couldn't figure out why Mildred had called such a small dog Prince, but it was her choice, and of course, since they thought she was a bit touched, they never mentioned it to her.

Betty shut the door behind her friends, turned and gazed into the emptiness of her home. It was times like this she wished she'd married. She heard a meowing from the kitchen—Safire, her Siamese. Betty gathered the teacups and headed for the kitchen. She leaned over to pet Safire, who arched up and began to purr. Maybe her cat missed the dogs coming over for a visit—believe it or not, they were the best of friends.

"This all you want, old girl," Betty said. The purr got louder.

The phone rang. "Who could that be?" Betty mumbled. "The only two people who call me this time of day just left my house…hello."

"Hello, is this Betty?"

"Yes."

"I'm John from Unique Gardeners. I believe your friends bought you a gift certificate to get your flower beds fixed up and I was just calling to set up your initial appointment."

"Bit quick on the draw aren't you, son?" Betty questioned.

"Well, your friends told me when they would be giving you the certificate…"

"I see," Betty said. "Well, I don't want you coming over tonight; I'm too tired now and I like to retire early."

"Not a problem, Betty—I may call you that?"

"Of course, it's my name."

"How about tomorrow morning, around 10:00?"

"I do my shopping on Thursday mornings at 10:00. How say we make it 8:00; I'm an early riser and I'll have my breakfast and dishes finished by then." Betty smiled. She was testing to see how ambitious this lot were—if they could be about business early in the morning.

"That will be fine, Betty; I'll see you at 8:00." The line closed.

"Well, what do you think, Safire, shall we read the paper before supper?"

Betty's forehead creased into a frown as she read the headline. This was the third bank robbery in a month and the police were unable to catch the culprits; the robbers didn't even show up on the security cameras!

"Strange," Betty thought, "there hasn't been a major robbery in this town for over 30 years."

Safire pushed her head against Betty's hand, ripping the newspaper. "Safire, look what you did—you tore the last paragraph of the story!" The cat jumped down and walked away in a huff.

Betty ate her supper and then took a walk to her back yard. It wasn't huge, but it was more than she could maintain now. She started to imagine how she would like it to look.

Betty hadn't slept well. She was uneasy about this gardening thing. The fellow on the phone had sounded pleasant enough, but she was remembering how Gwen and Mildred had described the shady characters waiting in the truck.

Safire followed Betty out to the front porch, jumping directly to the screened window, swatting at imaginary bugs in the dusty trail of sun's morning rays. Betty retrieved the paper, sat down at her little table, and turned to the front page. The recent robberies were playing on her mind. She wondered if there was any progress in catching the culprits yet.

POLICE ARE BAFFLED was the headline. Betty kept reading. She set the paper down and looked thoughtfully out to the street. Safire was swishing her tail and meowing loudly at the birds on the front lawn. Betty didn't let her outside; her previous cat, Ginger, had been hit by a car. She checked her watch: 7:55. A battered red truck pulled into her driveway and a nicely dressed young man got out.

"Hi, Betty," he greeted as he opened the door and stepped onto the porch. "I'm John, from Unique Gardeners. We spoke last night." He smiled—a charming smile.

"I know who you are, I'm not senile yet. Besides, the name is on the truck." Betty smirked.

John smiled—a tad artificial this time. "Do you mind showing me where you would like your flower gardens?"

Betty got up and headed for the door. "Don't let my cat out," she ordered. John followed, being careful of the anxious Safire, who arched her back and hissed at him.

As they entered the back yard, he smiled again, "Beautiful," he commented.

"Well, if it's so beautiful, maybe you don't have to do anything," the words were quick out of Betty's mouth. What was wrong with her, she wasn't usually this rude to people!

"Oh, I just meant that it will be a nice yard to work on," John returned. He looked around. "Those maples look old."

"Planted them myself the year I moved in, leaves are a pain in the fall, though."

John pulled a sheet of paper from his pocket and began sketching. "What are you writing there?" Betty queried suspiciously.

"Some ideas," he smiled.

"*He smiles too much*," Betty thought. "*Can't trust someone who smiles all the time*."

John walked the perimeter, checking the tall wooden fence. He turned to Betty as if he knew she was going to ask why. "Just seeing how strong it is for when we start digging," he smiled—again.

After about 20 minutes of sketching, John put the pencil behind his ear. "I think I have enough here to get started. Let's return to your porch; I'll show you some pictures and ideas for your yard."

Betty led the way. "Watch the cat," she reminded John as Safire made a dive for the door.

"I'll just grab my briefcase from the truck," John called out.

Betty scrutinized him carefully. There was something about him that left a creepy sensation in her bones. She observed him making a call on his cellphone, noticing his head bobbing up and down, and there was a bigger than usual smile on his face.

"Maybe he's had botox," she whispered to Safire, "and it left him with a permanent grin."

John shut the phone and joined Betty in the porch. She pointed to the table, then sat down and waited. He opened his briefcase and pulled out some catalogues. For the next half hour, he filled in his backyard sketches with flowers and bushes.

"I am aware you need something with little maintenance," he said at one point, "our company can also offer you a regular, affordable program so that you will barely have to lift a finger."

Betty was wary, "You just fix my garden with the amount of the gift certificate; I don't have money to pay your company to *maintain*," she emphasized.

John's lips formed a stiff smile. "Whatever you like, Betty," he said, patting her hand.

She pulled her hand away and checked her watch. "It's getting late; why don't you call me later with the final details and I'll let you know if I want to go ahead with it." Betty stood. Safire hissed at John from her window sill.

As John gathered his papers, Betty noticed his lips were smiling, but his eyes weren't. In fact, their blackness was tainted with anger. Eyes were something she'd learned to read well over her many years of classroom teaching.

"May I call you this afternoon around 2:00?" John asked.

"Make it 3:00; I nap at 2:00." Betty watched him get in the truck and throw his briefcase on the seat. She watched long enough to see him hit the steering wheel as he sped off down the road. "I'd give a penny or two for his thoughts right now," she commented to Safire.

John was angry. These old people were getting harder to manipulate, but he'd have to find a way to get through to this one—she had the perfect backyard!

After John had left, Betty poured a cup of tea and, while it was cooling off, decided to call Gwen.

"Hello," Gwen sounded sleepy.

"Gwen, I need to ask you about the certificate you and Mildred gave me. I didn't notice a dollar value."

"Well, that's because there isn't one," Gwen replied. "The fellow that sold it to us said we could get a complete garden makeover for a special low price, one only offered to seniors."

"How can they do that without seeing the yard?" Betty questioned. "There's something fishy going on here, Gwen, and I don't think I want this company poking their shovels into my yard!"

"Betty, Mildred and I paid good money for that certificate, even though it wasn't very much and I don't think…"

"Safire didn't like the man either," Betty informed.

"Safire doesn't like anyone," Gwen quipped. "Why don't you just get done what you want and leave it at that? Mildred and I just wanted to do something nice for you and you are still complaining!" Gwen added sharply.

"I'm not complaining about you and Mildred…it's this company…and the robberies that have been going on…we haven't had a robbery in this town for years."

"Oh for heaven's sake, Betty, get in the real world. I'll admit the guys in the truck were shady looking, but that doesn't mean they are bank robbers. Really now!"

Betty heard barking in the background. "Sorry, Betty, I have to go; Buster needs letting out. I'll call you later," Gwen said and then hung up.

As Betty gathered together her grocery coupons, she pondered on the situation. Safire was rubbing around her legs. "You don't get good vibes from that fellow either, do you, my pet?"

Safire meowed quite loudly.

In the meantime, John was explaining the situation to his partners at Unique Gardeners. "We are going to have to be cautious with this one; she's pretty sharp. I think she liked some of my ideas, but she was a tough old bird to read. The two who bought the certificate would have been better candidates, but they don't have the yard we need."

"Well, we know that she is an early riser and that she goes to bed early. We know she shops on Thursday mornings at 10:00 so that will be a perfect time for us to bring in the *special* plants. Did you find out anything else, John?" A sharply dressed, middle-aged man sat in the chair across from John.

"Actually, I did, Mr. Fornam. She naps around 2:00 in the afternoon and she has a Siamese cat, which I have the feeling does not like strangers!"

"Ah, Johnny boy, puddy tat doesn't like you?" a scraggly character jeered from the couch.

"Shut up, Ace," John threw back. "I've heard about Siamese; people say they are like a watch dog."

Mr. Fornam spoke up: "Does she let the cat out?"

"No, actually she doesn't; she was quite adamant I not let it out!"

"Good." Mr. Fornam turned his attention to the couch, "Ace…Mac…get the truck loaded for the next job. John, you make your call to Betty this afternoon and see if we can get started tomorrow?"

"I never got to finish the entire plan. I'll…"

"Finish it before this afternoon. Buy her a nice present, something that will reach past her crustiness—maybe something for her cat." Mr. Fornam frowned. "We need to pick up the pace a bit. I thought coming to a hick town like this would be easier, but so far it hasn't been. Are you losing your touch, John?"

"No, sir."

Mr. Fornam turned to Ace and Mac, "I heard you guys were spreading dollar bills around last night down at a local bar; I told you never to do that in the town we are at. I don't want to have to tell you again!"

"Yes sir," was the simultaneous reply.

"Okay—good—I am happy everyone understands; you've all got your instructions. No more sloppiness, not at this stage of the game!" Mr. Fornam stood and walked to the front door. "I'll be back tomorrow night and I expect to hear some better news."

As Betty was driving home from her shopping, she happened to notice the Unique Gardeners truck sitting in a driveway. She slowed down, just in time to see a well-dressed, middle-aged man exit the house and get into a silver Lincoln. As she continued on her way, Betty's imagination zoomed into full gear.

At three o'clock that afternoon Betty's door bell rang. She was quite angry when she saw who her visitor was. "I told you to *call* me at 3:00," she commented sharply. "Besides, I've changed my mind about the entire garden thing…"

John's face was not a happy one as he pushed the door open and stepped inside. "I don't think you want to do that," he smirked, "at least not without me showing you the plan," he added—with a smile.

Gwen meant to call Betty at noon, but she'd gotten busy with some scrapbooking and lost track of time. She knew better than to disturb her friend between 2:00 and 3:00; Betty was like an *old she-bear* if her nap was interrupted. Gwen checked her watch: 4:00. She picked up the phone and dialled Betty's number. After ten rings, Gwen's brow furrowed worriedly. "That's strange," she mumbled, "I wonder where she is?"

John left Betty's house with a big smile on his face. She'd signed on the dotted line and his gardening crew would begin their work first thing in the morning. Of course, she'd had no choice but to sign if she ever wanted to see that blasted cat again!

He'd arrived at Betty's house at 2:30 while she was still sleeping. John had picked the back door lock and stepped inside. The cat, which had been munching on kibbles when the door opened, had arched her back and hissed at him. Then, the nervy cat had started inching toward him, but he'd been ready. He threw the bag over her head, scooped it up quickly, and headed for his truck. He could feel the cat struggling and was thankful for the thickness of the burlap material.

John had taken Mr. Fornam's advice and bought something for Betty's cat, but of course, it was not exactly what his boss had in mind. John considered himself a genius at figuring out ways "to get the job done."

Betty couldn't believe what had just happened! She'd known. She'd told Gwen just this morning that she didn't trust this company, and her friend had told her how foolish she was. Now Safire was kidnapped and Betty couldn't even call the police or that horrid man might kill her! Betty's jaw quivered, but she clenched her teeth to head off the flow of tears. She'd figure out a way to get through this and those gardeners would answer *big time*—and, even *bigger time* if there were one hair on her precious Safire out of place.

Gwen decided to call Mildred, thinking they should go over and see what was going on with Betty. Maybe even take the dogs today; she knew Buster had missed seeing Safire yesterday. "Strange," she mumbled, "how the animals got along, especially when Safire treats the dogs with such disdain!" She knew Betty didn't eat until 6:00, so thought to pick up some already cooked chicken and potatoes from the grocer. Mildred answered on the third ring and when she heard the concern in Gwen's voice, she agreed it would be a good idea to check things out, and have supper together at the same time. She also agreed it was a good idea to bring the dogs.

As the two friends pulled into Betty's driveway, they were startled that the curtains were already drawn across for the night. That was not like Betty; she never closed them until after supper. Gwen and Mildred snapped the leashes on Buster and Prince and then headed for the door. The dogs were barking excitedly. Gwen was holding the bag of chicken; Mildred pounded on the door. They waited for what seemed like forever before Betty answered. The sight of their friend shocked them both!

Betty opened the door only a crack, and she kept her chain lock on. She looked as though she had been crying, and she was already in her housecoat. Betty never got ready for bed before supper unless she was feeling poorly.

"Let us in, Betty," Gwen demanded.

"We brought over some supper," Mildred added.

"Why didn't you answer your phone at 4:00?" Gwen questioned.

"I was not feeling well," Betty returned sharply. "Can't a woman have any peace without her nosey friends bothering her?"

Gwen noticed Safire was not at the door. That darn cat never missed an opportunity to try and escape. "Where's Safire?" she questioned.

"On my bed. Now, ladies, I truly appreciate your effort here, but I really am not up to company right now," Betty conveyed. "I want to get better before tomorrow because those gardeners are coming to start the yard first thing in the morning."

"I thought you were going to cancel the whole thing?" Gwen quipped.

"Don't want to waste a well-earned dollar," Betty muttered. "Now, I'd thank you two to leave me be. Enjoy your meal." With that, she shut the door.

"Something's not right here," Gwen stated.

"Should we call the police?" Mildred suggested.

Gwen snorted. "Mildred, that would be taking it too far. We'll just come over in the morning and see if Betty is in a better mood."

"Everything in place for tonight?" Mr. Fornam enquired.

"Right on schedule," John replied.

"No more problems with the old bird?"

"No, she came around quicker than I thought she would—even signed a regular maintenance program. We start on her yard first thing in the morning."

"Perfect," Mr. Fornam grinned. "Let's move out; after tonight's job we can just concentrate on our gardening for a while."

The night didn't go well for John, Max, and Ace. Mr. Fornam must have forgotten to block the cameras at the bank, but

Max had caught the security guard in time, just before he was about to activate the alarm. The only problem now, though, was that somehow they had to dispose of the guard's body!

And the cat…John cursed under his breath, just thinking about it. He'd taken Safire out of the bag to put her in a cage, and she'd clawed him a good one. Just as she dropped to the floor, Ace had come through the front door, and the cat had escaped into the night.

"Didn't know you had a cat," Ace commented. "Want me to run after it?"

"She's not mine," John had retorted angrily. "Maybe a car will hit her so I don't have to put up with her anymore—the nasty beast she is!"

"Oh, I see," Ace nodded his head, suddenly comprehending who Safire was. "So that's how you got the old lady to sign on the dotted line?"

John was irritated. "She'll never know I don't still have the cat; besides, that cat won't find its way home from here…"

"I've heard animals can find their way home even when they are dropped thousands of miles away," Ace butted in.

"That darn cat isn't that smart!" John returned. "Right now we have more pressing matters to think about. What's happening with the body?"

"Max is fitting it inside the burlap around the Mountain Ash tree root; we'll plant it right in the centre of the old lady's yard."

"We weren't planting a…"

"We are now," Ace grinned. "Just tell her that you decided to make a few changes. We'll make up a beautiful flower bed all around its base," he added.

"And the money?" John asked.

"Just where you suggested, no change in its location," Ace replied as Max walked in. "All done, buddy," he put his arm around Max. John didn't like the way Ace was taking charge.

"Yep, that guy will neva see the light 'o day agin!" Max laughed, showing off several black teeth. John cringed.

"Good man," Ace slapped him on the back. "Let's all get some shut eye; we have an early morning," he added. Ace and Max headed off to their rooms.

John stayed behind, brooding. He was still ticked with the cat and the way things had gone with the job. He also pondered on why Fornam hadn't blocked the cameras—he'd be questioning him about that in the morning! Good thing he'd had the foresight to grab the tapes.

Betty was restless. Sleep just wouldn't settle on her. She missed Safire. She sat up in bed and turned the television on. Maybe there would be an old movie playing that she could fall asleep watching. "I'm sure you'll find a way home to me if you can," Betty reached over to her nightstand and caressed the picture of Safire. "You are the smartest cat I ever owned!"

The morning sun reached through the cracks at the edge of the bedroom curtains, tickling Betty's eyes open. She glanced at her clock—already 8:30. The morning news was playing on the television.

...another bank robbery last night, only this time, the night security guard, Mal Carson, is missing and the tapes from the cameras have been removed. A blood stain at the scene has led the police to believe that there is foul play here...

Betty jumped from her bed and moved quickly to the window. She peeked, through the curtains, into her back yard.

What in the world were her two friends, and their dogs, doing here so early? Gwen and Mildred never rose before 9:00 a.m. Then, she noticed the gardening crew. What were they doing digging a large hole in the centre of her yard? That hadn't been in the plan!

Betty didn't even change out of her night clothes! She headed out to her back yard. "Stop!" she shouted to the gardeners. "Who said you could dig a big hole in the middle of my yard?" She turned to her friends. "And what are you two busy bodies doing here so early?"

Before they could respond, Ace sauntered up to Betty. "John asked me to inform you that he'd made a couple of adjustments to the plan—said you wouldn't have a problem." He paused, then stepped closer to her, sticking his face just inches from hers. "You *don't have a problem*, do you, Betty?" he whispered gruffly.

Betty backed away. The stench of a cheap cigar and whiskey was thick on his breath. "No," she garbled. "I don't have a problem."

Max finished digging the hole for the tree. "Ace, man, give me a hand with the tree, would ya—it's pretty heavy."

Ace threw Betty another grin. "It'll be the best garden you ever had," he said before going to help Max.

As the two gardeners dragged the tree over to the hole, Prince and Buster began barking ferociously at the burlap bag covering the roots.

John had sent Max and Ace on ahead to get started on Betty's landscaping, and to bury the body before it began to smell!

"Why were the cameras on?" he demanded to know from his boss.

"Must have gotten the wires crossed," Mr. Fornam replied.

"We were lucky Max caught the guard just as he was about to activate the alarm. Max went a little crazy, though—hit him too hard…"

"You didn't clean up your mess; the police found blood at the scene. I hope none of it belongs to you guys." Mr. Fornam pointed to the scratch on John's arm.

"A cat."

"You have a cat?"

"No!"

"Ah…so that is how you got the old woman to sign for the maintenance program?"

John nodded.

"Nice work. Well, by summer's end the heat should be died down on the robberies. You guys can dig up the loot when putting the garden to bed for the winter. Where did you say you were burying it?"

"I didn't."

Fornam glared at John.

"Under the gladiolas."

"Smart."

"I thought so. Glad bulbs have to be dug up in the fall."

"Can't you control Buster and Prince?" Betty demanded.

"Something about the tree they don't like," Gwen speculated.

"Oh, Gwen, it's only a tree; the boys are just excited to be here. By the way, where is Safire?" Mildred asked.

Betty's stomach waved with nausea. "Sleeping," she replied curtly.

Gwen was annoyed. "Maybe if you invited us in for breakfast, Betty, the boys could play with that lazy cat of yours."

"Safire isn't lazy."

"Well, she is…"

"Why don't you two just take your dogs and go eat somewhere else!" Betty snapped. She turned and noticed Ace wheeling some boxes over to the back corner. Max was finishing up around the tree. "What's in those boxes?" she queried.

"Gladiola bulbs," Ace grinned.

"I didn't ask for Glads."

"John has it on the list."

"When is John going to be here?"

"Soon."

Betty turned and stomped into the house. Her fingers hovered over the phone. How she wanted to call the police. What were these men up to? Why was *her* back yard so vital to them? Why did they have to kidnap Safire? And, oh how she hated being so brusque with her best friends, but she didn't want them to get hurt. Betty sat down on her couch. The floodgate opened.

She awoke to loud meowing. "Safire?" she muttered, heading for the door. And there she was—Safire—alive, and demanding to be let in! Betty opened the door, and Safire rushed in and began rubbing around Betty's legs. Betty had never heard Safire purr so loudly. Betty thought for a moment, and then picked up the phone and dialled.

"Hello."

"Is this John?"

"Yes."

"Betty, here…Your boys have left, and they left quite a mess—I don't like messes. I was wondering when you were coming back to finish the job?"

"How say, around 3:00, so as not to disturb your nap."

"You'll be coming, I hope; I need to discuss some things with you."

"Yes, I'll be there."

"Good." Betty hung up, smiled, and then made two more calls.

At 3:00, The Gardeners arrived. At 3:05, Gwen and Mildred arrived with the boys. It was a joyous reunion at the house at 42 Huddle Street as Buster and Prince licked Safire all over. Betty filled her friends in on the events of the last 24 hours.

Another car pulled up and parked across the street from Betty's house. Two suited men came up to her door, flashed their badges, and stepped inside. Betty motioned them toward the kitchen: "You can observe from there." She turned to her friends. "Well, girls, shall we take the boys out for some fresh air? I think Safire could use some as well."

The ladies headed outside with their pets. Buster and Prince made a beeline straight to the tree and started digging. Safire saw John and began growling and hissing!

"Get those animals away from here!" John ordered as he tried to shoo the dogs away. Buster and Prince began nipping at his pant legs.

And then Betty let Safire go. The cat instantly leaped onto John's back. He cursed when he saw her, and then screamed as her claws ripped through his shirt! The police officers rushed out the back door and headed off Ace and Max's departure.

The police Captain shook Betty's hand. "You're a brave lady," he acknowledged.

Betty smiled. She was remembering the stunned look on the faces of the gardeners when the police had dug up the tree and found the security guard's body. She was remembering their shocked expression as the bags of money were found under the Gladiolas! She could have carried, in a basket, the number of Glad bulbs they'd planted—she wouldn't have needed to wheel them in! But the best moment was John's face when he saw Safire—it was the look of utter defeat! It hadn't taken long for John to give up his boss, Mr. Fornam, the owner of one of the town's security companies.

"Shall we go out for supper, ladies?" Betty smiled at her friends and patted her purse. "It's on the police force tonight!"

Rodney

The only trace left of Rodney was two tiny running shoes scattered on the road. Melissa, his mom, didn't understand how not one person on such a busy street hadn't seen what happened. Rodney was never far from her side and she'd only turned her back for a few seconds.

"Who would do a thing like this?" she asked.

"Do you live with the child's father?" the police officer questioned.

"Of course." Melissa didn't understand why the officer had ignored her question.

"Good marriage?"

"What are you getting at?" Melissa demanded. "What does my marriage have to do with Rodney's abduction?"

The officer cleared his throat. "We have to ask these kinds of questions; too many times children are abducted by an estranged parent."

Melissa calmed down, realizing it was just routine questioning. "We've been married ten years and our marriage is just fine."

"Rodney your only child?"

"Yes."

"How old is he?"

"Three."

"Waited a while to have kids, eh?"

"John didn't want children at first," Melissa informed.

"Oh, why was that?"

"He came from a family of ten; said he wanted peace and quiet when he grew up."

"What made him change his mind?" the officer was studying Melissa carefully.

"Me. I convinced him one child wouldn't be too disruptive to our lives."

"Was he?" the officer's brows rose questioningly.

Melissa didn't like where this was going. She'd have to be careful not to say something incriminating about John. The officer didn't need to know John wasn't much of a father to Rodney—*an inconvenience* he referred to him as.

"No," she answered, "Rodney is a perfect child—quiet, bright, obedient…"

"John feel the same way?" the officer's eyes were too penetrating.

"Of course," Melissa retrieved a picture from her purse. "This is Rodney on his last birthday," she handed the photo to the officer.

Officer Brent Campbell studied the picture. The child could pose for cherub pictures, he was so beautiful. The curly blond hair tickled the nape of his neck; his eyes were large and the deepest blue Brent had ever seen; his skin was milk-white and his lips formed a perfect rosebud. If he didn't already know Rodney was a boy, well…

"Hello?" Melissa snapped, "Shouldn't you be getting an all points bulletin out for my son before something worse happens?"

"Of course, after a couple more questions—where is John now?"

"Out of town; he travels a lot for his job."

"Have you contacted him?"

"I left a message on his cell."

"As soon as you hear from him I need to know."

"No problem."

Melissa knew she wouldn't wouldn't hear from John anytime soon. He'd left a few nights ago—said he regretted his decision and didn't want to be a father and had given her a choice, him or the kid. She had angrily informed him it was a bit late for that ultimatum. John had stormed out of the house and she hadn't seen him since.

Brent had been a police officer long enough to know when someone was lying—Melissa was definitely not being truthful. Rodney's face would end up on a milk carton and on posters at the local department stores, but he would probably never be found. Brent picked up the picture, "I'll be right back."

Brent leaned back in his chair. He was a captain now, but he'd never, over the past 20 years, gotten Rodney's picture out of his mind. The boy was still missing.

Melissa, he'd heard, had a mental breakdown and was institutionalized. He had no idea where the father was. The guy had been a real cold number—just like he'd figured. Hadn't been able to pin anything on him, though—he'd had an airtight alibi.

Brent glanced out his window. It looked windy outside but Brent decided to walk home anyway. He'd take the route by the university to see if he could catch his daughter, Alicia, between classes. She'd been secretive about something lately—probably had a boyfriend, even though she knew how he felt about her getting involved with someone before she finished her degree.

Brent stopped in his tracks when he saw Alicia coming toward him on the sidewalk. A young man with curly blond hair, large blue eyes, milk-white skin and rosebud lips, accompanied her. "It can't be," Brent whispered, "not after all these years."

"Dad!" Alicia ran up to him, dragging the young man with her. "I want you to meet Allan; he is new at our school—

you won't believe the things we have in common!" she said excitedly.

Brent shook Allan's hand. "Nice to meet you." He paused, studying his daughter's friend. "You look familiar…"

Allan laughed. "Nice to meet you, too, sir; I've heard a lot about you." There was a mischievous curl to his lips. "You know, there is a lady at the hospital where I'm doing my internship—a patient—she thinks I look familiar, too—calls me Rodney all the time. I think she's taken a shine to me. Alicia and I delighted her with some flowers yesterday." Allan smiled.

Brent smiled back. Some things had a way of working out—eventually.

Rodney's Return

Captain Brent Campbell couldn't understand life's twists and turns. How was it that his daughter befriended the boy who had haunted his dreams for 20 years, or that this same boy was working at the hospital where his birth mother was institutionalized?

Brent was sure Rodney, known as Allan to his daughter, Alicia, had no knowledge of a prior life. What a break if he could finally discover what had happened. He picked up the phone and dialled Alicia's number.

"Hello," she sounded sleepy.

"Did I wake you?"

"No—what's up, Dad?"

"I'd like you and Allan over for supper Friday night."

"What's the occasion?"

"Just thought it would be nice to get together before the holiday," Brent stated. "I figured you guys would have 'young people' plans for New Year's Eve."

"We'd love to come for supper Friday. We'll be spending New Years at the hospital where Allan volunteers, though. He thinks it's more important to spend time with those less fortunate than to party with a bunch of strangers."

"Anything in particular that he likes to eat?"

"No, he's not picky. What time?"

"Five-thirty, okay?"

"See you."

Friday night arrived and Brent still hadn't figured exactly what angle he was going to use to get the information he needed. The table was set, the chicken and potatoes were in the oven, and a salad was in the fridge. A bottle of white wine sat in an ice bucket. The doorbell rang.

"Hi, Dad!" Alicia burst into the house. "Sure smells good in here; Allan and I are starving!"

Allan smiled. Brent noticed a healthy pinkishness to the white skin. "Yes, I'm famished; Alicia dragged me out skating all afternoon." Alicia gave Allan a gentle punch.

The evening passed quickly. "Goodnight, Dad; it was lovely," Alicia hugged her dad.

"Mr. Campbell, do you have plans for New Year's Eve?" Allan asked.

"Not yet."

"How about joining us at the hospital?"

Brent smiled. "Love to; what time?"

"Show starts at 8:00."

Brent dialled the number for Allan's parents.

"Hello," a woman answered.

"Hi—Mrs. Carmichael?"

"Yes, who's calling?"

"Brent Campbell. Your son, Allan, is a friend of my daughter. I would like to meet with you and your husband."

"Is Allan okay?"

"Yes, I just have some things we need to discuss."

Brent drove to Barrie and met with Allan's parents that afternoon. He hated what he had to do, but Melissa deserved to know her son was alive, and the boy had a right to know who he really was.

On the return trip, Brent was overwhelmed with what he'd learned. The Carmichael's were hesitant about talking at first, but after he told them Melissa's story and showed them Rodney's picture, they relented.

They had been living in Vancouver at the time of Rodney's adoption. They'd never had their own children and because of their age, adoption agencies always passed them over. Then a friend told them about a private agency that could get them a child as long as they had enough money. Before long, a young boy became available—Rodney. Of course, they'd been told his parents had been killed in a car crash and there were no known living relatives. They had moved to Barrie when Allan was sixteen. They were in total agreement with Brent about what had to be done.

Brent had a gut feeling who was responsible for Rodney being stripped from his mother's arms. Back at the office, Brent pulled Rodney's file, made a phone call, and a few minutes later a young officer came into his office.

"What's up, boss?"

Brent passed the officer a picture and a sheet of paper. "This man needs to be picked up and brought in for questioning on a cold case file. He slipped through my fingers 20 years ago, but I have proof now."

"Proof of what, sir?"

"That he kidnapped and sold his son."

Brent was buzzed into the psychiatric wing. He'd decided to wait until later to talk to Allan. He noticed Melissa right away.

"Hello, Melissa."

She looked up. "Do I know you?"

"Brent Campbell; I handled your case 20 years ago."

She smiled sadly and looked away. "Yes, I remember you now." She paused. "He's back you know—my Rodney. Works here. Doesn't know me, though. Says his name is Allan."

Alicia and Allan entered the room and asked everyone to take their seats. The show began. Brent observed the happiness in the room. As Allan prepared for the finale, Melissa suddenly stood up and started singing a lullaby about a boy named Rodney. When Brent glanced up at Allan, he saw the look on his face.

Allan began walking toward Melissa. His hands reached to her outstretched fingers. "I know that song," he whispered, tears filling his eyes. "Someone used to sing it to me." Melissa nodded, smiled, and kept singing.

Brent walked over and put his arm around Allan's shoulder. "I must speak with you, son; there is something you need to know."